Finding REFUGE

LUCY FRANCIS

Mini Gray Moose Publishing

Finding Refuge

Contact Information: kissybooks@yahoo.com

Cover Art by Lucy Francis.
  Images from:
  © Diego Cervo / Bigstock.com
  © Randy Hines / 123rf

ISBN-13: 9780615723808
ISBN-10: 0615723802
Publishing History
First Edition, June 2012

Mini Gray Moose Publishing
South Jordan, UT

Published in the United States of America

Dedication

For my editor, Trish, and my reader, Kim. Ladies, you rock!
I literally could not do this without you.

Chapter One

Travis Holt sat in his truck, eyes closed, fingers clenched around the steering wheel. Melancholy seeped out of the prison inside him and he brutally shoved it back into place. Lunch hadn't helped his mood any, but it didn't really matter. He faced several hours of work before the day ended, checking on various jobs in progress, meeting with an inspector for a final punch list, ensuring everything stayed on schedule. It all had to get done, and the rest of the world didn't care if he was having a lousy day.

A gentle breeze wafted through the half-lowered window, brushing over his face and ruffling his hair. He drew a deep breath of air touched with the scent of warming earth. The smell of spring that was so late in coming this year. He missed the way things used to be, when spring arrived on schedule in March, and summer was in full bloom by the time the end of May rolled around. June was always hot when he was a kid, but the last several years in Utah had seen snow in the mountains and cold, wet weather in the Salt Lake valley until the middle of June.

He hated it. Just one more frustrating thing in his life that he couldn't control. The misery he'd carried with him all day squeezed him hard, and he opened his eyes and fought back: turning on the truck, cranking up the stereo, heading for the next stop in his packed Monday list of crap he had to do. Thinking about the past didn't do him any good at all. Neither did the present, really, but at least if he stayed rooted in the here and now, living moment by moment, the knowledge that he was a failure didn't swamp him completely.

He sang with the rock song pounding through the speakers, distracting himself from the weight of his life. Because the awful truth nagging at the edges of his thoughts was that he'd reached the limit of what he could carry. One more thing dropped on top would push him under. He'd drown. If he didn't acknowledge that fact, he'd make it through every day, no matter what hit him.

Travis pulled into the driveway of the sprawling, French Country-style mansion sitting high on the Mount Olympus foothills. His client had spent a hell of a lot of money for a spectacular view lot, and Travis believed the man truly got what he paid for, with the primarily glass rear of the new house facing the valley. As he exited his truck, he noted the vehicles of the plumbing and electrical subcontractors parked on the drive. He crossed the path through the newly landscaped yard to the covered front porch.

His parents would have preferred he live in a home like this, ideally near them in Federal Heights. But he'd never give up his little chalet in Midway. The mountain town gave him room to clear his head. Living there, even with the daily commute, kept him sane.

Travis walked into the high-ceilinged, stone-paved foyer. Plastic sheeting covered the floor, protecting it from dirty workboots. Martin Delgado, the job supervisor, stood beyond the foyer in the open, airy sitting room, talking on his cell phone. Travis waved, and Delgado quickly ended his call.

"Hiya, boss," Delgado said, clipping his phone onto his belt.

"Are we on schedule?"

Delgado snorted. "Of course, man, you think I'd let you down?"

Travis smiled. "Good, because I'm talking to Mr. Jasper five times a day, and if this place goes into overtime, I may strangle him before he ever gets the keys."

"I feel for you. It's almost done. Rachel's putting up the fixtures and plates and Harley is just about done with the finish plumbing."

"Okay. I'm going to have a look around so I can tell Jasper I was here in person, and everything's fine."

Delgado laughed and reached for his phone when it beeped. "You do that, Travis. I'm glad I'm not you."

Yeah. Being me is even less fun that it looks. Travis went up the wide, lavishly milled, curving stairs, meaning to give the house a look from the top floor down. His intentions flew out the nearest window when he walked into the master suite and found himself staring up at the most perfectly curved rear-end he'd ever seen poured into faded denim. Sweetly rounded below a narrow waist, it was the sort of ass that women were forever trying to work off even though men begged for more.

He refocused, shaking off the buzz of appreciation zipping straight to his groin, and forced himself to take in the whole picture. The woman stood too far up for safety on a six-foot ladder, facing the opposite wall. She twisted a light bulb into the pewter fixture on the coved ten-foot ceiling. His gaze wandered up to dark brown, wavy hair. Pulled into a ponytail at the nape of her neck, the waves cascaded down the length of her red t-shirt, swaying at the top of her hips. He'd expected to find Rachel Garrett, his electrician. This tiny, curvy thing was definitely not Rachel.

"Who are you?" he asked.

She didn't respond. He stepped forward. "Are you here with Rachel?" He reached out and tapped the heel of her red tennis shoe. "Hello?"

She jumped at his touch, turning toward him as she took a hasty step down.

Her foot missed the ladder rung.

Travis reacted instantly, catching her as she fell, stepping back so she didn't hit the ladder.

A surge of fire blew through his system on the heels of the adrenaline rush, the heat pulsing through his chest as he held her, as his mind identified where he ended and she began. One arm held her around her waist, the other wrapped across her legs below her hips. For a moment, she stayed where she'd landed, half over his right shoulder, then she straightened. That position brought her breasts to eye-level. Her t-shirt, caught between them, molded against her, making it damn near impossible for Travis to swallow.

Heart pounding, Travis forced his gaze upward, meeting her dark brown eyes. The confusion in them threw ice water on his hormones. Small hands pressed against his shoulders and he loosened his hold on her, trying to ignore his physical interest as she slid down his frame to the floor.

She backed away a step, her gaze on her feet, her cheeks dusted pink, and pulled earbuds from her ears. The music blared through them. Ah. She hadn't heard him.

"Hey, sorry I startled you," he said. The rest of his words died in his throat when her gaze lifted and she smiled. A sweet, welcoming smile that lit up her entire self. It slid down inside him, stunning him and leaving a trail of light. No one he'd ever known had a smile like that.

"It's okay. Thanks for catching me before I hurt myself." She hitched her thumb over her shoulder at the ladder. "Guess I should have taken the 'do not stand on this step' warning seriously, huh?" Her voice was low, with a slight whiskey-rasp.

It was a punch to the gut after anticipating that she'd sound like a little girl to match her small size. She couldn't be more than, what, five-two? A grin spread across his face, he couldn't help it. "Pretty sure the warning is there for a reason. Are you here with Rachel?"

"Yeah, I'm visiting her, and attempting to help, though I clearly have no clue what I'm doing." She shrugged. Her smile faded and the part of Travis that had revived inside because of her smile died again, too. It stung. How could he fix that? "You were doing great, I messed you up." He held out a hand. "I'm Travis Holt."

Her handshake was surprisingly firm. "Andri Miller."

"Andri? Interesting name."

"Short for Andromeda. I know, I know, my mother is Greek, so I come by it honestly," she added hastily as his smile widened.

"No, it's a beautiful name." The sweet blush colored her cheeks again and his stomach flip-flopped.

Her gaze shifted to the right and she said, "You about got me killed, sending me up on a ladder like that."

Travis turned to see his electrician walk in. Rachel Garrett, dark red hair looped through a Dodgers cap, looked Andri over. "You appear unscathed."

Andri pointed at Travis. "Thanks to the hero."

A sharp jolt of pleasure hit him. He'd love to play the successful hero again, anytime. He bit down on the thought that her need for a hero was his fault. Always his fault, but he refused to let his failings shadow her words.

Rachel stood beside him, tall enough to meet him eye to eye. "Yep, that's Travis. He spends his copious spare time rescuing damsels in distress." She nudged him with her shoulder, and that contact from his lifelong friend snapped him out of the magnetic pull emanating from Andri.

Shaken by his reaction, he steeled himself and glanced at his watch. "Unfortunately, speaking of spare time, I have none. Rach, you'll be finished today?"

"Yes. Another half-hour maybe, and we're out of here."

"Just what I wanted to hear, thank you." He nodded at Andri. "Nice meeting you."

She smiled as she said goodbye, but he yanked his gaze away from her. That smile was kryptonite, best avoided since he couldn't hope to fight the way she drew him without even trying.

He did a high-speed check of the rest of the mansion, pausing only to confer briefly with Delgado. The plumber had already finished and gone. Inspection complete, he beat a hasty retreat to the truck.

Andri. He'd known Rachel forever and never run into this friend of hers before. She'd said she was just visiting Rach, so chances were he'd probably never see her again. And while that realization pained him, it also relieved him.

There were two kinds of women. Those who played, and those who didn't. Andromeda Miller was decidedly one who didn't. She sent off waves of home and hearth and 'till death do us part' vibes. Absolutely off-limits, and he knew precisely why—stability was the one thing he needed, the one thing he wanted. The one thing he didn't deserve.

It was also a hell of a catch-22. If she wasn't what he thought, well, he'd paid the price for mistaking a player for a stayer before, with his ex. And if she really was what he read her to be, a good girl…damn, he couldn't go there. He'd only end up failing her somehow, like he failed everyone else, and in the process, she'd learn to hate him. He knew if he ever saw that light in her eyes replaced with hatred, it would utterly destroy him.

One more thing added to the pile. No. He simply wouldn't allow himself to go there. Period. No matter how much he wanted to cling to the lifeline her smile had thrown him.

* * * *

Andri stared out the electrical van window as Rachel drove away from the mansion, the finish work complete. She twisted a lock of hair around her finger, not really watching the passing landscape. These quiet moments did nothing to help her escape the swirling soup of self-doubt threatening to swamp her lately. She hated feeling like this, lost, unsure. And now, oh, what those amazing blue eyes had done to her.

"Hey," Rachel said, her voice gentle. "I was willing to let you stew while we finished up back there, but we're facing a twenty-five minute drive home, give or take, so now would be a good time to talk."

"Talk about what?" She'd shown up on Rachel's doorstep in Park City late last night after a brutal twelve hour drive from Phoenix, and her sweet friend had been content to show her to the guest bedroom and let her crash. This morning, she'd woken up just in time to get cleaned up and hop in the van to hang out with Rachel as she worked. She hadn't expected to end up helping her friend work. Which brought her thoughts firmly back to the ladder fiasco. Every nerve ending from head to toe sang at the feel of his hard muscled arms wrapped around her...

Rachel sighed. "Come on, woman, how long have I known you?"

"Ages."

"Yep. So talk to me. You're all thoughtful over there. You'd better not be mooning over that cheating SOB you left in Arizona, or so help me—"

Andri held up a hand, shaking her head. "No, absolutely not. I don't waste my time thinking about Pete."

"Good. I seriously thought about hopping on a plane and giving him a piece of my mind in person when he did that to you. Still not sure how you never figured out he was seeing someone on the side, though."

Andri shrugged. "Easy. I'm stupid."

Rachel shot her a stern look. "No."

She sighed. "Oh no? He was seeing another guy, Rach. And I didn't see it. I'm pretty sure that qualifies me as stupid."

"No. Naïve, maybe. He showed you an orthodox, traditional guy, and you believed in him."

"I thought he was being a gentleman. I mean, my mom introduced us, and she met him at church." She'd been swept away by his refined manners, his kindness and thoughtful things he did for her. He knew so much, had so much culture, and he'd never touched her in lust. That should have been a red flag, but it was so refreshing and old school and romantic. To realize that the flowery poetry he'd written had been composed while thinking of his boyfriend just slammed her self-esteem into the dungeon and tossed away the key.

She shrugged, tracing a finger absently along the window seal. "Maybe if I hadn't been working such long hours, I would have put it all together sooner. I don't know."

"I still think you should have outed him."

Andri shook her head. "There was no reason to be cruel to him. Honestly, I can't imagine living in that kind of hell. He's so ashamed, so afraid to be who he really is. He has to find a way to deal with that or be stuck in his own personal perdition forever. At least I could walk away."

Rachel took a long look at her. "I don't know how you do that. You get hurt and you find a way to understand the guy's motives and even feel sorry for him."

She slumped in her seat and blew out a breath. "Hating him for it won't make me feel any better. You know, I was going to marry him under false pretenses of my own. I mean, he offered me so much, such stability. That's what I wanted. I was so tired of being alone and having my mother constantly complaining that I was going to be single forever. I didn't love him, not really. We both made bad choices."

And now she had to live with knowing that the only guy who'd ever wanted to marry her had been looking for a beard. Was she that undesirable that only a gay man would want her in his life? Even worse, she'd almost stayed. Almost let her need to nurture and rescue condemn her to living the rest of her life permanently lonely in a sexless marriage.

She shook off the dark twist of her thoughts and shifted in her seat to focus on Rachel, instantly her friend the day they met in the U. of U. dorms as freshmen. It didn't matter that they'd lived in different states since college. Rach always had her back. She smiled. "Thanks for letting me visit you. I really needed a place to go, some time to clear my head."

"Well, I'm thrilled to have you. And, you know, Ian won't care because he's hardly ever home."

Andri nodded. Rachel's pro skier brother had always seemed like a decent guy. Too bad she couldn't have fallen in love with him, but there was no chemistry there at all in the few occasions she'd spent with him.

Rachel glanced over her shoulder and changed lanes. "So, what did you think of Travis? Not exactly how I ever pictured you meeting him." She laughed, a full, clear sound.

"Yeah, falling into his arms. Probably the strangest way I've ever met someone." She closed her eyes for a moment, recalling the thrill that shivered down her spine at the feel of his strong arms around her, hot on the heels of the fright of falling. His solid shoulders beneath her hands, his body heat setting all her nerve endings on alert…

"What did you think of him?"

Andri pulled herself out of her thoughts. "Well, the photos spoke the truth."

Her friend muttered something about the idiot driving too slow in front of her, then said, "Yep. Decent eye candy, that man."

"Very true." His image rose in her mind, standing beside Rachel back at the mansion, matching her five-ten height. Not huge, but still far taller than she was. When he'd caught her, time had slowed and she'd found herself staring at him. His short brown hair had sun streaks and tiny lines showed at the corners of his amazing dark blue eyes.

What bothered her wasn't how he looked. It was how he looked at her, at least for a moment there. His eyes had filled with surprise when he caught her. Of course, she'd only imagined the flicker of interest in his gaze before he set her back on her feet. But when she smiled at him, something shifted behind his gaze. The walls there dropped, just for a moment, giving her a glimpse of darkness swiftly eclipsed by his answering smile.

Something about that flash of deep-seated pain behind his smile had reached out and grabbed her by the heart. And that was all she needed. Pain in others had always called to her, spiking the soul-deep desire to rescue and soothe and heal.

But she'd learned a harsh lesson from watching her parents. You couldn't build a relationship on one person saving the other, because you ended up with one person sucking the heart and soul of the other dry, never changing, leaving only a husk where the nurturer once was, useless to themselves let alone anyone else.

Rachel slowed the van as traffic thickened in front of them on the canyon interstate. Probably an accident up ahead. "I think you should go out with him."

Andri's mouth dropped in shock. "What? No!" Her stomach flip-flopped, setting off her anger. She was not doing this. No way. And not just because he was suffering. The only man who'd shown more than fleeting interest in her since college ended up being gay. Clearly she had no man skills.

Raising a hand, Rachel said, "Now, just wait a sec and listen. I'm not suggesting a relationship."

"Good. Not ready to do that." Especially after she'd already had an emotional and physical reaction to Travis. Though, in all honesty, couldn't part of it just be due to loneliness? She'd probably have reacted strongly to anyone who smiled and treated her like he'd noticed, and been interested in, the fact that she was female.

Rachel snorted. "He's not ready, either. Look, I've known Travis most of my life. I absolutely adore the man. But he deals strictly in temporary arm ornaments since his marriage ended. Emotional involvement just isn't going to happen. I know you're not doing the emotion thing either, and let's be honest, dear friend, you would make a lovely ornament."

Andri felt the blush stain her cheeks. She gave herself credit for being reasonably pretty, but an ornament? Um, no. "So...what? You're suggesting that I date him for entertainment?"

"Sure, why not? It would be good for you. He's interesting, heterosexual, and a lot of fun to hang out with, and I think you could use some fun while you're here. Who knows, you might even get lucky." Rachel slid her sunglasses down and wiggled her brows.

An unwelcome thrill shot through her at a sudden vision of kissing Travis. He did have nice, well-shaped lips. Andri shoved the thought out of her head. "You are impossible."

"That wasn't a no."

Andri sighed. "I'll think about it." Dating wasn't even on her radar at the moment, but maybe one date, just for fun, wouldn't hurt. As long as it didn't go anywhere. And as long as she never again saw the pain crammed inside him.

Chapter Two

Wednesday morning gave Travis a taste of the summer heat he craved. Too bad he only had a moment to enjoy it. The apartment door opened and the stench of the place swallowed Travis as he stepped inside. The odors of sweat, cigarettes, beer, some painfully floral perfume, and apple cinnamon air freshener clung to him. Jeez, thirty seconds into this, and he already needed another shower.

He eyed the skinny blonde with the bloodshot eyes who let him in. Where in the hell did Danny get his taste in women? "Where is he, Misty?"

She waved a hand in the direction of the hallway. "Back there, in my room, the one on the left. I'd let him stay, but I gotta get this place cleaned up. Landlord called, said he's coming by today to fix the sink. He'll have a cow if he sees all this."

Travis stepped over empty beer cans and vodka bottles littering the ugly brown shag carpet. Misty didn't stand a chance in hell of cleaning up anything if she was as wasted as she looked. He worked his way back to her bedroom, trying to breathe only through his mouth.

Danny lay sprawled face-down on the floor. Travis nudged his brother with his foot. Danny shifted slightly and mumbled a foul curse at him.

Travis focused on the ceiling, gritted his teeth, mentally ticked off the numbers from one to ten, trying to get a grip on the anger rising in his chest. God, he wasn't up for this today. He was too damned tired after spending the past couple of nights tossing and turning. He was accustomed to the jumbled stew of work and bad memories that usually crossed his mind at night, but his dreams had added a new torment: a curvy little brunette with incredible hair, a gorgeous ass, and big, expressive brown eyes.

He dropped his gaze back to his brother. "Come on, Danny, I've got things to do."

He stirred. "Go away. I'm totally wasted and I swear, if I move, I'm gonna throw up."

So much for being on the wagon. Travis looked around, and felt his tenuous grip on his temper slip when he spotted a mirror on the bed. A mirror holding a short straw, a credit card and a few streaks of powder. Dear God, not again.

He reached down and clamped his hands around his brother's arms, hauling him to his feet. True to his prediction, Danny heaved. Since he was facing the other direction, Travis simply waited until his brother finished emptying his gut on that lousy carpet before dragging him outside the apartment.

He pulled Danny out to his truck, then turned him around and pushed him hard against the passenger door. Travis bracketed his hands on Danny's face, examining his reddened nose and bloodshot eyes. He didn't miss the stray wisps of white powder under his nostrils.

Heat flushed Travis's face, and his hands trembled with the force of his anger. "Damn you, Danny, I thought you were clean. Misty said you were drunk, and that was bad enough. But this? When did you start using again?"

His brother squinted at him in the bright morning light. "Oh, hi, Trav. Sorry I was an asshole, I didn't know it was you kicking me around back there."

Travis fisted his hands in Danny's shirt, if only to keep from beating him to a bloody pulp. He checked his volume before he spoke again, in an effort not to create too much of a scene. All he'd need right now was someone in the apartment complex hearing a fight and calling the cops. "How long have you been back into the coke, Dan?"

Danny cracked the grin that helped him seduce dozens of women. He shook his head, his long black hair falling in his eyes. "I don't know. What day is it?"

With a growl of frustration, Travis released his brother and paced away a few feet. Twice he'd put Danny in rehab. Twice. It obviously wasn't working, and the helplessness made his head spin. If his brother's latest girl hadn't called Travis to come get him...

Travis eyed Danny's low-slung red motorcycle a few parking spots away. How long would it be before he tried riding that thing strung out? At best, he might get pulled over for driving under the influence and end up in jail. At worst— no, he didn't want to think about the worst.

He turned back to Danny, who had slumped down against the truck and was steadily sliding toward the pavement. Travis strode over, yanked his brother up, opened the door, and half-pushed, half-lifted him into the passenger side of the truck.

Travis stalked to the rear of the truck, lowered the gate, and slid a long board into position as a ramp. He reached back into the cab, fished through Danny's pockets until he found the keys, then took his brother's beloved crotch-rocket rumbling up the makeshift ramp into the bed of the truck.

The deep growl of the engine made the bike feel like a big animal beneath him. Something not quite trained, that would turn on him the minute he relaxed. Danny liked it because it felt wild and free to ride. Danny was too wild by half without the help of the stupid motorcycle.

Travis's chest ached, tight with frustration. He gave the bike's tie-down straps a harsh yank, hoping to release some of the stress. This couldn't keep happening. His brother had only been out of rehab for a month this time. Danny's savings was cleaned out, and he wasn't working even part-time hours for the company.

God only knew how much money he'd blown on drugs and alcohol in the last few years. He couldn't continue feeding his addictions without cash. Somehow, though, Travis doubted a lack of funds would bring Danny's drug use to an end. He'd find a way. The little bastard could be incredibly resourceful. A supply of cocaine was probably the source of Danny's attraction to Misty.

Travis climbed into the truck cab and looked over at his little brother. Danny leaned against the door, his head rolled to the side against the back of the seat. His cheekbones seemed sharper, his face looking more gaunt. Damn, he looked older than twenty-five. Travis sighed and leaned forward, setting his forehead against the steering wheel. Danny's addictions were aging him, too.

It would be a great help if, just once, his parents put in some effort to take care of his brother, rather than turn a blind eye to their youngest son's problems. Yeah, and maybe some sweepstakes folks would show up on his doorstep with an oversized check for a million bucks.

He sat up and started the truck. The flames of his anger had ebbed, leaving him cold and dark inside. He pulled out of the parking lot, debating where to take Danny. He glanced at the dashboard clock, then reached over and shook him by the shoulder. "Hey, Dan."

He yawned. "What?"

"Can I leave you safely at home or do I need to take you to work with me so I can babysit you?"

Danny gave him a dark look. "Travis, I'm exhausted and I feel like shit. Take me anywhere you want. All I'm going to do is sleep."

Travis's knuckles tightened on the steering wheel. "How many days have you been up?"

Danny rubbed his eyes and yawned again. "I went to a party at Jared's on Saturday."

Saturday. He shook his head. "Daniel, today is Wednesday."

Silence filled the cab as he concentrated on driving. Just when he was certain his brother had fallen asleep again, Danny softly said, "I'm sorry, Travis."

The anger tightened into a protective hurt. "This has to stop."

"I know."

"If I take you back to your place, will you promise to stay there?"

"Yeah. Do you need me on the job tomorrow?"

"I always need you on the job."

"I'll be there, Travis. Clean and sober. I promise."

Travis got Danny to the bed in his townhouse and unloaded the motorcycle, then turned his focus to his mental to-do list as he left. He waited for a break in the traffic, then pulled into the lane for the freeway onramp. He needed to go into the office today, but he couldn't work all these emotions out of his system sitting at his desk. He bypassed the freeway entrance and turned at the next traffic light, heading for the nearest job site.

He knew better than to let Danny's moment of remorse in the truck count for anything, even if it was the first time he'd apologized for the drugs. Just because Danny recognized he had a problem didn't mean he had the strength to avoid temptation. There had to be a way to help him, and he'd find it.

He had to. The price of failure was way too damned high. He could barely live with himself after losing one brother. To lose the second? No. Never, ever going to happen, no matter what.

Travis grimaced. He should have taken the business trip to Colorado when Dad gave him the option. It would have saved him from so much. Danny. Mr. Jasper pestering him about the house.

A crystal-clear memory of catching Rachel's friend, Andromeda, slammed into his thoughts. He shook it off, unwilling to give thoughts of her devastating smile and equally impressive curves any more time. Bad enough that she'd invaded his dreams.

He forced his brain back to the Danny issue. It might have done Dad some good to retrieve Danny from the hole of an apartment where his skanky girlfriend lived. Maybe it would open his eyes. Confronted with Danny's substance abuse that blatantly, how could Dad continue to avoid the subject?

That's exactly what he'd do, send his father next time. As much as he hated to think it, there would be a next time.

Travis blew out a long breath. He'd feel better after he pounded some nails. Nothing could reach him when he worked. Not paperwork. Not Danny. Not pretty women with mythical names who he'd never see again.

* * * *

Andri stood by the Garrett Electrical van, adjusting the thick coil of insulated copper wire on her shoulder. She breathed deep, letting out a contented sigh as she turned her face toward the sun. It was much warmer today, though the air was still cooler here than in Arizona.

For the last couple of days, she'd gone to work with Rachel, playing gofer, and she found herself appreciating the routine, so different from her usual one. In Phoenix, she'd grab a piece of toast on her way out the door in the morning, then put in ten hours or more at work, dealing with network installations, systems malfunctions and end-user meltdowns, followed by on-call emergencies once she got home. She'd squeezed in time here and there to attend business functions with Pete and managed to catch an uninterrupted movie once in a while.

Rachel's more relaxed life had already forced her to slow down, to remember how to breathe. The difference in her tension level amazed her. She was sleeping far more than usual, working on eliminating the severe sleep deficit she'd accumulated over the last few years. She even tried out Rach's unhurried breakfast routine this morning, enjoying the eggs and hashbrowns she'd cooked up.

Andri looked around at the condominiums under construction around her. A few units closer to the road, near the *Silver Meadows by Holt Construction* sign, were completed and up for sale. Rachel had parked in front of a framed building of four joined units. "So what's the plan today?" she asked as Rachel handed her a staple gun.

"Rough electrical. Lots of drilling, setting boxes, running wire." Rachel filled the pocket of her toolbelt with nails, then grabbed another coil of wire, a drill, and a bucket of outlet and switch boxes. "You can staple the wire unless you'd rather relax and read. Totally up to you."

Andri lifted the staple gun in a salute. "I can handle stapling. Lead the way."

She followed Rachel up the makeshift front steps of the first condo unit, pausing when she heard the rumble of a pickup truck pulling in by the framed building south of where she stood. She turned and a delicious shiver coursed down her spine when she saw Travis Holt climb out of the big black truck. Shoot, what was he doing here? Didn't Rachel say he was running the construction company with his father? Yet there he was, buckling a tool belt around his narrow hips. Wait, he was here to work, hands-on?

She wanted to walk up the steps and into the condo before he glanced her way, but her feet were glued to the wood beneath them. And then she no longer wanted to move. Travis stripped off his shirt in one graceful, mouth-watering motion. A tingle started low in her belly. It radiated outward, weakening her knees. He wasn't built bulky. His muscles were lean, layered on by hard work. He slathered sunscreen across his bare skin, muscles sinuously shifting under the tanned surface. Her fingers itched with the urge to help him lotion his back.

He pulled on a black White Sox cap and climbed the stairs into the building. After a moment, she spotted him moving through the bare roof trusses with the other men on the framing crew, nail gun in hand.

Andri swallowed hard. Great. He'd be right where she could see him at a glance, laying plywood for the roof. How was she supposed to concentrate on helping Rachel when he was out there, the sun glistening on his bronzed skin?

She had promised Rachel she'd think about going out with him, but, oh my, thinking about him at all could get seriously out of control now. She shifted the wire coil on her shoulder and trudged into the building. Even if she could keep herself from looking out the windows every five minutes, it was going to be a very, very long day.

* * * *

Travis loved hauling a nail gun around, forty feet above the ground, the sun spreading warmth across his skin as he secured sheets of plywood on a dramatically pitched roof. Nothing else forced him to live completely in the moment the way roofing did. Under those conditions, thoughts of anything outside work fled. His focus was simple. Get the work done, don't get killed. One wrong step, one slip, was all it took at this height.

He concentrated on the position of his feet and the balance of his body weight. The pine scent of the wood engulfed him. He heard only the staccato pounding of the framing crew's guns blowing nails into boards.

Work. Just work.

He didn't want to think about the paperwork piling up at the office, or his intense frustration with Danny.

He didn't want to think about the darkest brown eyes, or long, thick, wavy hair, or that low, grainy voice.

He shoved everything aside. After a while, nothing reached him but the work. Hard, methodic, muscle-killing labor.

The morning flew by, and when Travis paused to pull his ball cap off and run his hand through his damp hair, he noticed the other guys were heading down for lunch break.

He left his cap by the nail gun and walked across the roof. He swung down through the trusses and dropped to the floor ten feet below, then pounded down the temporary stairs to the ground floor. Outside, the men who brought their lunches to the site sat on stacks of plywood and two-by-fours, eating in the slight shade cast by the tall buildings.

"Hey, Travis!"

He turned at the shout and saw Rachel Garrett emerge from the open doorway of the unit across the walkway. She waved, beckoning him as she walked to her van, so Travis obliged and trotted over. "What's up?"

Rachel grinned at him. "You just coming down for lunch?"

When he nodded, she said, "Come on, join me and Andri. We brought plenty of food today."

"Andri's here?" His stupid heart jumped just saying her name. He clamped down on his reaction.

"Yep, she's playing gofer girl for me."

No, Travis. His stomach growled. Hey, it was just lunch with a couple of friends. What could be the harm? "I don't even care if you brought chick food. I'm starving."

Rachel grimaced as she opened the van and reached for the cooler. "Oh, please, when have I ever eaten chick food?"

"Let's see, what grade were you in when you were crushing on my cousin, Alec? Tenth?"

"You're seriously bringing that up?"

He laughed. "Yeah, and you were so worried he'd think you were a tomboy that you wore a dress to the Memorial Day picnic and picked at a teeny little salad when all of us knew you would have killed everyone there for a steak."

She swatted his arm. "And you let me think he liked me even though he had a girlfriend, jerk. How does leftover chicken and potato salad grab you?"

"Works for me."

"Good." She pressed the cooler against his chest until he took it from her.

Travis followed Rachel inside to the open kitchen area, where Andri knelt on the wood floor, smoothing out an old blue blanket. She looked up, glanced from him to Rachel, her brows rising in some unspoken question.

Rachel hitched her thumb at him. "Company for lunch." She took the cooler from him as Andri's gaze connected with his. For a moment, she hesitated, her expression unreadable. Then she smiled, and his knees went a little weak. He grinned back. Damn, she was so pretty. And that smile pulled at him, hard, making him fight to remember why she was supposed to be off limits.

Travis lowered himself to the floor across from Andri as Rachel dug in the cooler, handing him plates and forks. He set one of each in front of her, then reached out, offering a set to Andri. "I wasn't expecting to see you on the job."

"I'm becoming quite an efficient little helper." She took the plate, her fingertips grazing his knuckles, sending awareness zinging through his hand, up his arm, coursing through him.

Man, he was on really thin ice if he got a thrill from a tiny touch like that.

Rachel nodded, handing Andri a bowl of potato salad. "You are a good helper, and I like bossing you around."

Andri giggled, and the rich, textured sound poured through him, burning into his stomach. Yep, he had it right the first time he saw her. Kryptonite. This was a woman who could strip him to the core without even trying. He turned his attention to filling his plate. He needed a change of subject, had to focus on something, anything besides Andromeda Miller. "Rach, how did your parents enjoy their anniversary cruise?"

"Loved it. If they could afford to spend retirement on a ship full time, they probably would."

He laughed. "Sounds like Uncle Mac. I haven't seen your brother in months. Is he still working on his degree?"

She shook her head. "Nah, he didn't have enough time for it. I don't think Ian will go back to school for real until his ski career is over. He's been smart with his race winnings, plus he doesn't pay rent, so he can be a bum for a few years, even if it all ended tomorrow. He's such a brat."

Andri said, "Doesn't that drive your parents crazy, watching Ian play for a living?"

Rachel reached for chicken leg, a broad smile on her face. "Oh, it might look like he plays, but he works incredibly hard just to stay in fighting shape."

The three of them talked lightly through lunch, discussing the weather, sports scores, world news. Finally, Rachel stood up, leaving her empty plate on the blanket. "Back to work for me, but don't you two run off on my account." She walked away, taking the stairs up to the next floor two at a time.

Travis took a deep breath as Rachel left, steadying the sudden staccato beat of his heart. What was left of his appetite vanished the moment he found himself alone with Andri. She set her own plate aside as he watched her. For a moment, she looked down at her hands, pressed against her knees, then she started cleaning up, stacking the plates and replacing everything in the cooler.

He couldn't stop himself. "How long are you going to be here, visiting Rachel?"

She shrugged. "I'm not sure. A few weeks, maybe." She stood and waved him off the blanket. When he got to his feet, she picked up the blanket and folded it. "I'm sort of on vacation. Figuring some things out, you know?"

The grainy quality in her low voice touched something primal, deep inside him, hooking him, and for a moment, he wasn't sure he remembered why he should be fighting this attraction. "Would you have dinner with me tonight, Andri?"

Her eyes met his then, wide, turbulent. He got the distinct impression she was sifting her thoughts, making a measured decision. Then the turbulence cleared and she smiled. "I'd love to. What time?"

Travis broke into a grin. "Great, uh, six-thirty? I'll pick you up at Rachel's house."

"All right, that works. I'd better go help her, then. Make sure we're done on time." She gave him that brilliant, soul-warming smile one last time, then retreated up the stairs where Rachel had gone.

The lightness in his soul lasted until he crossed the walkway to his truck. His cell phone rang. He pulled it from his pocket, only to feel the waves crash against him. The caller ID said Craig Jasper. "Lord help me, this guy is going to drive me insane." He leaned against his truck, calmly answering his anxious client's questions. No sooner did he get the man off the line than his office manager called.

He glanced up at the unfinished roof, resignation settling on him like a blanket. He'd get no more manual labor today. He'd pushed aside his office duties as long as he possibly could, and now he had to pay for it. He waved at one of the guys on the crew, who grabbed his cap and tossed it down to him.

He talked to Peggy all the way to company headquarters in Fort Union, and it wasn't until he stepped into his private office and closed the door that it fully dawned on him what he'd done.

He'd asked Andri out.

He leaned against the door. What was he thinking? He never dated, except to functions where he was expected to show up with a woman on his arm. The only other reason to date was to find a companion, and he couldn't bring himself to try. The potential for pain to himself, or worse, for him to hurt someone else, was too great.

The memory of the way Andri smiled crept into his thoughts. Her bright, genuine smile warmed the dark places inside him.

She couldn't possibly be as sweet as she seemed. He could dig a little and find the negative traits he knew must lurk under the surface, the things about her that would turn off his response to her. They had to be there.

He'd had his libido under firm control for a long time, but she rattled him. The edges of his control slipped when visions of her flooded his brain. He would dissect her personality tonight and be done with her.

A nagging thought tickled his brain. What if she ended up being wonderful? That made his heart skip a beat, but he reined himself in. She didn't live here. She was a visitor, taking a break from her usual life.

Hmm. Maybe he should take advantage of that, enjoy her company a bit before she left. Either way, then he'd be able to let her go. She would be out of his head completely, leaving him to his comfortable, familiar misery.

Chapter Three

The doorbell rang at precisely six-thirty, and Andri panicked. She was ready. She had been for twenty minutes. Once she told her about the date, Rachel had insisted on taking off early and going shopping to be sure she had a great outfit. So here she stood, in a long, cream floral halter dress she'd fallen in love with, paired with navy sandals.

She still wasn't sure about her face. Cosmetics just didn't look the same on her as they looked on other people, but she'd done her best. Mascara, sheer powder, and, since Rachel had insisted, a matte rose lipstick, but she nixed anything else because more always made her feel like a little girl playing dress-up.

"You look fantastic, Andri," Rachel said, peeking around the edge of the kitchen doorway. "Stop stressing out in front of the mirror and open the door, or I'll do it for you."

She threw a pleading look at her friend and got a thumbs-up in return. She drew a deep breath. She looked presentable. This would be fine. She pushed her hair back over her shoulders and opened the door.

Travis stood on the front porch, his hands in the pockets of khaki pants. The rolled-up sleeves and open two buttons and the top of his pale green striped shirt gave her a glimpse of tanned skin and toned muscle. Ohhh, he looked good. She allowed herself a quick glance from the top of his thick, sunstreaked hair to the toes of his very nice leather shoes.

Something bright and hot sparked deep inside her when she realized his eyes were roaming across her in a slow, casual once-over. His gaze caught hers, and his lips curved into a sexy grin that stole her breath.

"You look great," he said. His silky baritone sent shivers up her spine, and she wondered if she'd be able to eat with the butterflies circling inside her. She'd give anything to know if she affected him like this, or at all. She did not want to be the only one chemically involved here.

She forced herself to breathe evenly. "Thanks, so do you."

He cocked his head slightly, his grin widening, deepening the crease of his dimples. "Thanks. Are you ready?"

Andri grabbed her purse and a cream wrap off the rack beside the door. "I am now."

She shut the door behind her and walked beside him to his truck. He opened the door and held out a hand to help her in. The touch of his calloused hand under hers sent a livewire shock through her body, tingling in the pit of her stomach.

She climbed in, and before she could tug her dress to safety, Travis tucked the long hem out of harm's way, then closed the door. The small act stunned her. Either he had been well-trained, or Travis possessed an eye for detail and a level of thoughtfulness she'd not seen in other men she dated. She hoped it was the latter, but she knew he'd been married before. What sort of woman had he chosen? She forced her thoughts away from that subject. Whatever woman she might imagine would instantly morph into everything she wasn't and further inflame the inadequacy festering inside her.

After he'd backed out of the drive and headed down the highway into Park City, he glanced over at her. "Do you have any preferences?"

"I'm not picky. Just feed me, I'm starving."

That brought his killer grin back. "I know a great Mexican place. Will that work for you?"

"Maybe. How's their chile verde?"

"Just the right amount of heat and the pork's tender, lots of flavor."

"Yep, that'll work." Her eyes drifted down his tanned arms, layered with corded muscle, to his strong hands gripping the steering wheel. Hands used to putting tools to work. She considered briefly whether his hands would be rough or gentle on her skin, then batted the thought away. In the first place, who's to say he even felt that kind of attraction to her. If he did, it would be fleeting. She'd had her first boyfriend in college and a few that followed. It never lasted long. One or both of them always lost interest after a month or two or three. None of her relationships had any staying power until Pete, but look how that turned out.

The restaurant was fifteen minutes from the house, and small talk about the weather and how their respective days had gone kept them occupied until they settled into a brightly striped booth, digging into chips, spicy salsa, and fresh guacamole.

After they placed their orders, Travis leaned toward her slightly, dipping a chip in salsa. "So, where are you from? How do you know Rachel?" The warm expression in his eyes encouraged her. He sounded genuinely interested rather than someone reaching for something, anything, to say.

"Originally, Colorado Springs. I met Rachel at the University of Utah when we shared a dorm. I moved to Phoenix after graduation, but we've stayed in touch."

"Ah, that's it. I wondered why I hadn't met you before, but while you two were at the U, I was at Clemson. What do you do?"

"I'm a computer geek. I ran the IT department for a grocery chain in Arizona. Now I'm between jobs."

"What happened? Did you quit?"

She thought she saw a hint of dismay in his expression. She understood. Walking away from a stable job in this economy did make her look like a flake. "I really needed to get out of Phoenix."

The dismay morphed into curiosity mingled with concern. "That sounds ominous."

"Not really. It was more a case of a lot of things that added up until I realized it was time for some changes in my life. I wasn't very happy with how things were going, so I gave my notice and got out of there after I'd shown my replacement around. Rachel kindly offered a place to crash while I get my head sorted out."

He took a drink of his soda, then leaned back in his seat, watching her. "There are days I'd love to do that. Just, step back, take an honest look at things, and make changes."

The conversation bounced around for a while until their meals arrived. Travis thanked the waitress at the same time Andri did, and she grinned at him. Her dad always said to watch how her date treated those who served him, because she'd learn a lot about his character. So far, so good.

As he cut into his smothered burrito, Travis said, "Tell me about your family."

Andri finished swallowing a bite of spicy but incredibly flavorful chile verde, then said, "I lost my dad a few years ago. Colon cancer. My mom lives in Phoenix. She'd moved there while I was in school, and she loves it there, loves the Greek community. My brother, Dmitri, is an attorney out in upstate New York. What about yours?"

"I work with my dad, I'm sure Rach told you that. He's the best."

She grinned, watching him dig into his dinner. The man ate with gusto. "Sounds like you have a good relationship."

"Oh yeah. You know, he always made time to do things with me, even when business was wearing him down. We'd go hiking, or take the boat out and fish. Sometimes, he'd pick me up after school and we'd sneak off to the movies together, just the two of us. Then he'd make up excuses about where we were when we got home late for dinner."

She laughed with him, delighted with mental images of him as a boy. She watched him eat for a moment while she devoured her own meal. He was a breath of fresh air, so amazingly...normal. Centered. Confident without being arrogant. A man who actually listened to what she said, who didn't just sit there waiting for her to stop talking so he could hear his own voice. Not to mention he was yummy to look at. So far, Rachel was right. This was fun. "Tell me about your mom."

His expression closed a bit, but the tone of his voice remained smooth. "My mother is a fine woman. She does a lot of work for the homeless and children's causes. Most of her time goes to charity work. Always has. Of course, now it's more in the form of organizing big affairs to bring in donations, but when I was young she spent time in the trenches, feeding people, helping them face to face."

"Wow. I've always admired people who give so much of themselves to others. What about siblings? Rachel said you have a brother."

The moment she saw the shadow flicker across his face, she regretted asking the question. She'd obviously hit a painful subject, and she didn't want to ruin the evening. Even more, she didn't want her nurturing instinct to kick in. "I'm sorry, Travis, I seem to have said the wrong thing. Forget I asked, okay?"

He raised his eyebrows, surprise registering on his strong features. After a moment, he gave her a slight smile. "No, it's fine. I do have a brother, Daniel. He's five years younger than I am."

"Are you close?"

"Yes and no. I boss him around more than he appreciates."

"That's what big brothers are for. Dmitri made my life miserable, but I sure miss having him around sometimes."

The conversation lightened up as they finished their meal. Travis paid the bill, then gently draped her wrap over her shoulders before they ventured outside. An evening breeze cooled the mountain air by a good twenty degrees, and Andri tightened the wrap around her.

They continued talking on the way back to Rachel's house, trading memories from growing up. Andri soaked it in, learning everything she could about this wonderful man before the evening ended. When they reached the farmhouse, he switched off the engine and shifted on the seat to face her. The evening light outlined his face, glinting in his eyes.

"So, I'm curious. You seem very together and on top of everything, and I can't figure out for the life of me what you're staying with Rachel to sort out. What drove you out of Phoenix?"

Whoa, that was a swerve into serious. Telling him about her sham of an engagement wasn't a conversation she really wanted to have, but there was no point in avoiding it, either. If he asked Rachel, she'd tell him. Better that it come from her. She toyed with the ends of her wrap. "Well…I was engaged."

His brow knitted. "Did you call it off?"

She nodded. "We shouldn't have been engaged in the first place, so I saved us both from a very painful future together. We would have divorced eventually."

His expression closed, his gaze hardened. Her stomach took a sickening dive. Now she'd done it. A ruinous end to an otherwise decent date.

"You decided to not even try to make it work?" Accusation simmered in his words, and she sighed, reaching for patience. Of course he would think the worst of her at this moment.

"Travis. He was gay."

His expression melted into compassion instantly. "Oh, damn. Wow. Not openly, I'm guessing."

"No. That's why he wanted me, to help provide cover."

"And you agreed to marry him?"

"I didn't know, at first."

"Oh. How long were you together before you figured it out?"

She felt the blush flow across her cheeks. "That's embarrassing. It took about a year."

Travis whistled. "I...at the risk of sounding unkind, um..."

Andri sighed. "Why did it take me so long? Didn't I notice that he had no interest in touching me outside of hugs and perfectly chaste kisses?" She pressed against the bitterness rising inside her. "Believe me, I've asked myself every possible version of the obvious questions and most of the not so obvious ones, too."

He said nothing, only reached over and took one of her hands in his. She realized then she was trembling. She never meant to have a deep conversation with this man, and yet, here she was, smack in the middle of one with no hope of a quick resolution. Nowhere to go but forward. "He treated me with perfect chivalry, and I assumed he was old-fashioned. I never suspected a thing until I discovered him enjoying a little afternoon delight with his boyfriend. I put the pieces together really fast after that."

He winced. "No wonder you needed to escape."

He caressed her fingers, offering a gentle comfort. The threat of impending tears stung her eyes and she blinked hard, swallowing them. She'd be damned if she'd cry. That would be a horrible way to end the date. There was something else she could do, though. Something that would offer as much comfort as shedding tears and do much to repair the tattered edges of her self-esteem. "Escape isn't all I need. I realize I've been used and walked on. I need to remember how to assert myself and make sure my needs are met."

Rachel was right. She needed some fun. And she needed a man to really look at her as a woman, if only for a little while. This man didn't want any entanglements. That made him perfect for this moment. She locked her gaze onto his as she reached up and drew her fingertips down the side of his face. His eyes darkened and he sucked in a sharp breath as she traced one finger over his lower lip. That was precisely what she needed most. His interest, that glint of desire in his eyes.

He swallowed, his voice rough when he spoke. "What do you need, Andromeda?"

She refused to stop and think. "Right this second? Travis, I need you to kiss me."

* * * *

Travis's logic raised its head for a split second, but she dropped her hand to his chest, her lips parted slightly as she drew a breath, and all that mattered was giving her what she wanted.

He leaned forward, sliding his fingers into her thick, silky hair, bracketing her face with his hands. Her gaze dropped to his mouth, then her eyes slid closed as he pressed his lips to hers. He kissed her gently, caressing her lips, soft and full beneath his own. His heart skipped with every hitch of her breath, and her hands glided over his shirt and up into his hair, encouraging him to deepen the kiss. He traced his tongue along her lower lip, and the whiskey sound of her low moan shot straight to his groin. She parted for him and he dipped his tongue into her delicious heat.

He pulled her into his arms, angling his head for better access as they explored each other, her tongue meeting his stroke for stroke, her little whimpers of pleasure tingling in his blood. Her hands trailed down his neck, flexing and kneading his shirt against his chest, sliding over his ribs to his back, urging him closer.

She tightened her arms around him, holding him, infusing him with her warmth, her sweet, small breasts pressed against his chest. In that crystalline moment, he connected with how desperately he needed to be touched. Followed almost immediately by the realization that he was a split second from groping a girl in his truck like some horny teenager. With a silent curse, he ended the kiss, pressing his lips to her cheek then holding her as their breathing evened out. Andri leaned back first, letting a little air flow between them. Her gaze churned with confusion, flecked with desire.

Then her expression cleared, as walls slammed shut behind her dark eyes. His own armor thickened in response. This wasn't going anywhere. Nor should it.

Andri smiled as they let each other go, separating without recoiling from each other. "Thanks, Travis. I had a great time tonight."

"You're welcome, so did I." He paused for a moment, searching for something non-committal to say, but it became irrelevant when she placed her hand on the door. The night was over. Travis shook his head and held up a finger to make her wait, then got out and jogged around to open her door.

His heart still pounded harder than necessary when he took her hand to help her down, her fingers cool in his light grip. He kept hold of her as he walked her to the porch, registering through the remnants of desire fritzing out his brain that she didn't make any move to pull away. No. There was nothing to this. It was friendly, that's all. A nice date, a new friendship begun, and friends held hands sometimes.

She stepped up on the stairs and faced him, closer to his height. She opened her mouth to speak when a car door slammed. He released her hand and looked over his shoulder as Rachel approached from the driveway, a grocery bag swinging from her hand.

"Hi, guys." Rachel edged around Travis and stopped on the stairs next to Andri. "How was dinner?"

"Great," Andri said. She smiled, the version that didn't reach her eyes, not the one that pierced the fog in his soul. He warred with the desire to fix that while a part of him sighed with relief. Easier to walk away like this.

"Yeah, good food, good company," Travis said, welcoming the easy exit Rachel's appearance created. He couldn't have Andri. Correction, he shouldn't. He never wanted his own heart ripped out again, but his top priority was ensuring he didn't hurt her either. "I'd better be going, Andri. I have an early day tomorrow."

"Thanks again for dinner. I had a good time."

"My pleasure." He nodded a farewell at Rachel, then retreated to the safety of his truck.

He cranked up the rock music on the way home, refusing to think about Andri. Once home, though, her image took up space in his head and refused to leave.

Travis sat in the dark, on the leather couch in the main room, staring up at the flood of blue light from the salt-water aquarium dancing on the ceiling. It had been way too long since he was genuinely attracted to a woman. So long that while his brain comprehended why he would never have a relationship with Andromeda Miller, his libido refused to accept no for an answer.

He'd forced himself away from her tonight, but getting close enough to touch her in the first place had been a less than stellar idea. It had been so damned long since he'd allowed himself the simple pleasure of a real kiss, and kissing her was so very good, but if he made the mistake of losing himself in her, he'd doom them both.

Everything inside him tightened a notch, still feeling her beneath his fingers. He wrenched his thoughts away from the screaming physical attraction and considered what he'd learned about her. He'd never known a woman quite like her. She'd surprised him, showing him traits he admired. Honesty, kindness, sensitivity to difficult subjects.

She gave the simple expression of a smile a depth and warmth he'd never seen. She talked about her broken engagement, clearly a painful subject, without calculation or guile. And, damn, that hadn't been one of his best moments, had it? He'd instantly judged her motives, assuming she wouldn't try to work things out before he had the slightest clue what had gone so very wrong for her. She had every right to hold his immediate accusation against him, but she hadn't. She just calmly explained.

He cursed himself and went into the office to check his email. So far, Andri was all those things he didn't want her to be, and that made it brutally difficult to get her out of his mind. He answered a couple of messages, his attention only half on what he was doing. He could all too easily picture her in his life, taking up residence in his home, in his bed. He couldn't go there. Did she want children? That question hadn't surfaced, though it wouldn't surprise him to hear she wanted a full house. God, he didn't need his imagination going there, but he couldn't yank his thoughts away, either.

He'd never have children. He didn't dare. It was bad enough to fail other adults in his life. It would break his heart to fail a child.

Andri deserved far more than he could give her.

Travis firmly placed her on his off-limits list. No matter how much his body craved her, he wouldn't allow himself to hurt her. He couldn't see her again. If he did, his desire for her might overwhelm his good sense, and then he would do something they'd both live to regret. He'd marry her.

* * * *

Andri sat at the heavy pine table in the farmhouse after Travis left, her brain—and her hormones—good and frazzled. She made a point of not thinking about him, about his kiss, while waiting for Rachel to find the ice cream scoop.

She loved this vintage kitchen. The old wooden cupboards retained their distressed look, and red gingham checked curtains and modern appliances in early American styles added to the feeling of homey, old-fashioned living. Someday, if she ever had a house rather than an apartment, she wanted a kitchen like this.

Rachel cheered with success and returned to the table with the scoop and two spoons in one hand, bowls in the other. She took a chair across the table corner from her. Andri reached for the shopping bag on the end of the table and pulled out the mint chocolate chip ice cream, then took the offered scoop and dished up a bowlful.

Rachel's green eyes glittered with that time-to-gossip look, but she said nothing as she scooped her own dessert. Andri sighed, letting a spoonful of ice cream melt in her mouth until her friend squirmed in her seat and tapped her fingers on the table. Curiosity was killing her.

"Oh, all right," Andri said. "I can see the suspense is getting the best of you."

"Can you blame me? Two of my best friends go out to dinner, and I have to hear about it secondhand, and you're not spilling."

"We ate at Tia Maria's Grill. We talked. He brought me home."

Rachel's eyes flashed with frustration. "No! I require details."

Andri indulged her, with tidbits from what they ordered to how he draped her wrap across her shoulders and some of the subjects of conversation. She found herself stopping short of revealing the intimate details of their conversation, like the way his expression clouded talking about his mom and his brother. Clearly, things were not all sunshine and roses in the Holt family.

The Garretts were close to them, so Rachel probably knew the details already. She could ask her to fill in the blanks, but decided against it. If she wanted to know more, she owed it to Travis to get details directly from him.

And she didn't want to know more, she was certain of that. Already she felt the pull to him, the desire to take care of him, to soothe away his hurt, waking and stretching inside her. She refused to make her dad's mistakes in her own life.

"Did he kiss you?"

She'd known that was coming. She did her best to look indignant and offended. "None of your business."

Rachel waved her spoon dramatically. "Hey, the man's got a mouth made for kisses."

A sharp tingle zoomed through her. Oh, God, yes, the gentle caress of his lips, the slow sweep of his tongue against hers, the way his hands tightened in her hair. She still felt the heat they generated, coiled in her core. "For someone who notices details like that, I'm surprised you've never kissed him."

Rachel made a face. "Gross. That'd be like kissing Ian. Besides, I'm turned on by a little more badass than Travis has in him. And tattoos are always a nice bonus. So, did he kiss you or not?"

Andri's cheeks heated and triumph crossed Rachel's expression. "Hah, I knew he kissed you."

"Once. Briefly." She had to stop thinking about it, stop feeding the desire to feel his lips on hers again.

"Liar. So, when are you going out again?"

Andri's heart flipped, and she forced herself to find calmness again. He hadn't said anything about seeing her again, which filled her with equal measures of disappointment and relief. "We're not. He didn't ask to see me again."

Rachel growled, annoyed. "Stupid man. I hate saying that, because I know he's not stupid. Look at you! You're pretty, smart, talented, fun to be with. What was he thinking?"

She appreciated her friend's support, but the more Andri thought about the evening, the better she felt that he hadn't asked her out again. She had too many things to think about right now to be starting a relationship. "Rach, you said yourself he's not looking for anything. Tonight reminded me that I'm not really ready to be dating, either. If he does ask, I'm going to turn him down."

"I don't approve of that plan."

Andri smiled at Rachel's reaction. She was a great cheerleader, but this wasn't something she could push her into. "Sorry to disappoint you, dear."

They had nearly finished the ice cream when Rachel's brother, Ian, walked into the kitchen, wearing biking clothes. The clingy yellow and black fabric showed off his lean form, hugging his muscular thighs and butt. With his fit body and attractive face, it's a wonder he didn't drag a horde of off-season ski bunnies everywhere he went. "Hello, ladies."

"Hey. Want some ice cream?" Rachel pushed the carton across the table.

Ian tucked a thick lock of dark red hair that had pulled loose from his ponytail behind his ear, then rummaged through the refrigerator, emerging with a plate of leftovers he put in the microwave. "Dessert comes after real food, Rach. How did dinner go, Andri?"

"Fine. Travis is a really nice guy."

He turned a penetrating gaze on her. "Then why are you drowning your sorrows in ice cream?"

She stopped herself before she denied it, because it had finished up that way. Well, not drowning sorrows so much as smothering desire, but the concept correlated. "I'm fine, really. He's easy to talk to, and we had a lovely time."

Ian leaned on the table, pushing his forelock out of his face, a concerned expression in his brown eyes. "He'd better have behaved himself. You're a sweet girl, Andri, and he's a bit of a player lately. Haven't seen him with the same girl twice."

Rachel snorted. "Travis is harmless. It's Danny who's trouble."

Ian nodded. "Fact."

Andri bit her tongue to keep from asking for details. She didn't want to get involved, couldn't let herself get wrapped up in whatever drama Travis was coping with in his family. She knew better.

The microwave dinged and Ian pulled his plate out. "Anyone want to come watch TV with me? I might even let you hold the remote."

Rachel agreed. Andri tagged along, glad for the distraction, and dropped onto one end of the family room couch. She'd enjoyed Travis's company, all of it, from the small talk to the searing heat of his kiss. But there was a whole network server full of baggage locked up inside the man, probably riddled with malware and viruses too, and she knew better than to let herself consider getting involved with him. She'd pay for it too dearly.

Chapter Four

"Earth to Travis."

He caught the sound of his father's voice at the edge of his thoughts and wrenched himself into the moment. Travis looked up, surprised to see Terrence Holt sitting on the edge of his oak office desk, a stack of papers clutched in his beefy hand. "Morning, Dad."

Terrence's salt-and-pepper brows knitted. "You awake today, son?"

Travis scrubbed his fingers through his hair and yawned. "I'm tired. Haven't been sleeping too well the last few nights." Especially last night. True to form, discovering Danny was getting into trouble again brought the dreams back. The anguish knotted around his heart and left him drained when he woke up. He'd kill for a solid eight or even ten hours, but he knew from bitter experience how many more restless nights he faced before his brain would finally let him sleep in peace.

His dad reached over and patted him on the shoulder. "Sorry to hear that. Did you notify all the subs about the change in start dates for the Bridlewood shopping center?"

"Peggy did yesterday." His office manager had kept his head above water here while he sorted himself out on the job. It was probably time to give the woman another raise.

"Good, good." Terrence surveyed the folders, plans and assorted paperwork filed by pile on the desk surface. "You're looking busy."

"I am, thanks for noticing."

"You ought to dish some of this off on Danny. Give the boy something a little meatier to do."

Travis leaned forward in his leather chair. "Is Dan here today?"

His father nodded. "Just talked to him on my way in here."

Well, that was a step in the right direction. Danny really had been more reliable since his last stint in rehab, up until this week when he fell off the wagon again. Maybe having to retrieve him from Misty's yesterday was a solitary blip on the road to recovery.

Travis cranked down on the relief trying to surge inside him. Much as his heart wanted to believe Danny was okay, his head knew better. Danny wasn't out of danger, not by a long shot. Still, his appearance in the office felt downright positive.

"I'm really glad he's here," Travis said. "Every time he doesn't show up, I panic."

Terrence shook his head and sighed. "Son, you have to stop that."

"Stop what?"

"Stop spending all your energy worrying about Daniel."

"He needs help, Dad."

"And you've given him help. But at some point, you have to let him live the life he chooses, Travis. He's going to do what he's going to do. You can't force him to live your way."

God, that was cold. Worse, it sounded like his mother talking rather than his father. "I can't let him self-destruct."

"You can't let your life hang in the balance of whether he decides to straighten up or not."

Frustration simmered inside Travis. "Well, he's here. I'll go put him to work."

"I need to get back to work myself." Terrence eased off the desk, then winced and put a hand on his chest.

Travis jumped up, a ripple of fear coursing down his spine, and grasped his father's elbow to steady him. "Dad, what's wrong?"

"It's nothing. I think I have a respiratory thing coming on. My breathing just gets a little tight lately, and it makes my chest hurt. I need to have Dr. Shandel call something in for me."

"You should probably go in for an appointment."

His father shrugged. "I just had a checkup six months ago, and I'm the healthiest sixty-four-year-old he's ever examined. But if the doc thinks he should see me, I promise, I'll go in."

Travis hadn't noticed quite how the years weighed on his father until that moment. Terrence Holt didn't hold his big frame quite as straight and tall as he had in his prime. His hair had thinned considerably and filled with white, all without Travis realizing it. He'd put so much energy into Danny that he hadn't spent enough time with his father lately. "Hey, Dad, I hear that new World War II movie is pretty good. Why don't we take off early one day next week and go see it?"

Terrence beamed at him, a wide grin showing the dimples Travis inherited. "Sounds great, son. How about Tuesday? I can clear my schedule if you can clear yours."

"For you, I'd cancel anything." Travis gave his father's shoulders a squeeze and watched him walk out the door.

Travis yawned again, running a hand through his hair. He added his father to the mental list of crap to worry about, then grabbed the roll of blueprints for the Okada house and walked into his brother's office.

Danny sat at his drafting table, leaning into his work as he sketched. Travis stepped behind his brother, watching the gorgeous facade of a Victorian-style house flow from Danny's pencil onto the paper. His brother had always preferred drawing on paper, even though nearly everything else he did was computerized.

Travis waited silently as his brother completed the act of creation. While Travis had skills, he was no artist. In addition to Mother's looks, Danny inherited her talent. Beauty, whether classic, modern or whimsical, sprang from Danny's fingers when he worked. Travis had long since outgrown his jealousy to become quite proud of his brother's abilities.

Abilities he hated to see thrown away when Danny's addictions got the best of him.

Danny finished and shifted to the left, giving Travis a better view of the creation. Two stories, dormer windows, scrolled gingerbread accents under the eaves and decorating the wraparound porch. Full stone front. Knowing Danny, the final layout would come in around eight thousand square feet above ground, plus basement. On a nice acre and a half or two…He did the estimate in his head. Two point five, maybe two point six million dollars worth of new Victorian luxury, easy.

"What do you think?"

Travis met his brother's gaze, saw the need for approval reflected in the deep blue. "It's beautiful."

His eyes lit up. "Thanks. I've been thinking about it for a while, wanted to get it on paper." Danny flexed his fingers and popped his knuckles, eyeing the roll of plans Travis carried. "What's up?"

Travis handed the blueprints to his brother. Danny slid his new drawing onto a wide shelf above the table, then opened the plans of a sprawling ranch house.

"Go to the main floor."

Danny flipped through the pages of elevations until he came to the main floor layout. He laid the plans on the table, using the clips at the top to secure the curled pages. His mouth pursed as he examined the plans, shaking his head. "What idiot drew these?

Travis laughed. "I thought that would be your reaction. The Okadas had them drawn up years ago, but now that they're ready to build, they want some changes."

Danny crossed his arms over his chest. "I should hope so. The design is terrible. There's no natural flow to the layout. They'll feel like rats in a maze, scurrying from room to room."

"Mrs. Okada wants a more open design, but I don't think she has specific ideas about how to change it. Will you meet with them and help them figure it out?"

"When are they coming in?"

"Whenever Peggy makes an appointment for them." Wait, maybe that was a bad idea. Travis added, "Or, do you want to call them?"

Danny's eyes darkened. "Afraid I'll space off an appointment, Travis?"

Travis met his gaze directly, sliding into his business mode in an effort to keep emotion out of the argument he felt brewing in the air. "It wouldn't be the first time."

His brother picked up his drafting pencil, twirled it around his fingers. "I won't fail you. I mean, I'm here, aren't I? I promised I'd be here today, and I am."

Travis bristled inside at the defensiveness in Danny's voice. "Is that what I have to do? Make you promise every day that you'll be here the next? Will that keep you out of trouble?"

Danny laughed bitterly. "That's rich. When did you and Dad switch roles? He's just happy to see me when I come in, but you come down on me like I'm a teenager you've caught sneaking into the house after curfew and smelling like beer."

Travis drew a deep breath, steadying his temper. "I dragged you out of that foul apartment yesterday. You're fresh off a four-day bender. Now I'm supposed to take your word for it that you'll actually come in and earn your salary?"

His brother's jaw ticked and if he hadn't been so angry, he would have withered under Danny's glare. "I made a mistake, Travis. One mistake. Yeah, I fell off the wagon. You have no idea how ashamed I am, and how much it bothers me that I can slip up so easily. I don't need your guilt trip when I can put myself on one so well."

They stared at each other in silence for a moment, the tension weighing heavily in Travis's lungs. Finally, he leaned forward and clasped his brother's shoulder. "I know you're trying, Dan. Are you taking your antidepressants?"

Danny cursed. "I hate those things. They wipe me out. And they're drugs, too, you know. All I'm doing with that shit is exchanging an illegal fix for a legal one. It isn't a real solution, it's a crutch."

"There's nothing wrong with using a crutch until you heal."

"Speak for yourself."

Travis stepped back, loosening the tension between them with space. "Fine. Do you want Peggy to set up an appointment with the Okadas?"

"Yes, whenever is convenient for them." Danny paused, then said, "I'm here to work, Travis. I'll do my job. Trust me."

Travis left Danny's office and stopped by Peggy's desk long enough to ask the grandmotherly woman to take care of the appointment. He closed his office door behind him, then stood by the windows and stared out at the mountains that bordered Salt Lake City. He clenched his fists, then relaxed them purposefully, trying by force of will to unwind the tension in his muscles. *Trust me.* He wanted to, so much that his chest ached and his shoulders were rock hard with the strain.

Unfortunately, he knew better. Damn, it hurt to recognize that he couldn't trust his brother. He'd hope for the best with Danny, all the while waiting for the other shoe to drop.

* * * *

The next several days ran smoother than Travis expected. Unfortunately, that left him with a lot of time to think, and what kept surfacing in his otherwise orderly thoughts was a curvy little thing with gorgeous hair, an incredible smile that filled him with sunlight, and a kiss that made him hard if he thought about it too long.

One week after he'd taken Andri to dinner, he checked the schedule to figure out which jobsite he'd have to visit to run into Rachel. If Andri was still in town, she'd probably be on the job, playing gofer. Stupid as the idea was, he wanted to see her again. So he'd called her. She didn't answer and she didn't return his call. He'd texted. Nothing. And damn, rather than being smart and taking the hint with a huge sigh of relief, he'd found himself more intent on seeing her again. *Stupid.*

He left the office for a late lunch and drove to a custom home under construction in Draper. He went through the house, anticipation winding through his gut, until he spotted Rachel running wiring on the upper floor. "Hey, Rach."

She looked up from pulling wiring through the hole into a box. "Hey, yourself. I'm a little miffed at you."

He leaned against the door jamb. "What did I do now?"

"Oh, no," she said, pointing a staple gun at him. "It's what you didn't do."

Ah. That was it. "I didn't call Andri." Well, he had, but nothing had come of it. To Rachel it would probably be the same thing.

"He shoots, he scores. So, what, you didn't like her, maybe because you have the brains of an amoeba?"

He hated it when she got snippy with him. She was the annoying sister he never had. "Of course I like her. Where is she?"

"Doing something besides being my slave girl. You didn't call. I hate guys who don't call."

Arguing that he had, in fact, called wouldn't help him. She was on a roll. "Does she want me to call?"

She grumbled under her breath. "No, but that's beside the point. She likes you, but she's kind of a mess right now, not that she'll really admit it."

"Want me to be honest with you?"

"Why is that even a question? Lay it on me, Travis."

"I like her. A lot. I want to see her again." His heart pounded, a sudden trickle of fear slithering down his spine at admitting how he felt. "I don't think she'll let me."

Rachel stopped working and faced him squarely. "Why would you think that?"

"Hmm, I don't know, maybe the fact that she won't answer my calls or texts."

"That's bad for the ego. Didn't know she was serious."

"Serious about what?"

She waved a hand, pursing her lips. "Nothing. Listen, I like you, most of the time, so I'll throw you a bone. Of course, you have to know what to do with said bone when it lands in your lap."

"I'll figure it out. What do you want me to do?"

Rachel, bossy thing that she was, gave him a perusing look. "Get your hair cut, it's way long. Then, I expect to see you at my house for dinner. We're eating a bit late, be there by seven."

The fear flashed again, with hope hot on its heels. "Am I bringing anything?"

"A cleaned-up version of what I see before me should be sufficient."

He had to be out of his mind. This could only end badly, for both of them, but in this moment, he understood the meaning of hope springs eternal. A spark of optimism deep inside him chanted *what if?* Maybe he was a glutton for punishment, already seeing the likely ending, the heartbreak, looming before him if he took this path, but that spark pulsed bright and he had to chase it. "I'll be there."

* * * *

Andri sat part of the way out of the back of her car, taking off her sandals. She tossed the sandals over her shoulder, hearing them slap against the opposite door as she slid her feet into the new waders she'd bought yesterday. She slipped her boots on, then stood, sliding the waders up over her shorts and t-shirt until she could pull the suspenders over her shoulders.

She looked down at herself and grinned. Sky-blue waders, what an excellent find. She'd only found khaki and hunter camouflage before, and, ugh. Really? If companies were going to bother making waders for women, they could at least run with the concept and make them pretty. After all, the fish didn't care what color she wore.

She'd considered hip boots, but the one time she'd tried fishing a river in hip boots, she'd stepped into a deep spot and ended up drenched to her waist. Better to stay dry when the water was still runoff-cold. She turned the dial on each boot to tighten the laces and popped the trunk to get her gear. Well, Rachel's gear. Hers sat in her mother's closet in Phoenix. She slid the pack from the rod tube and unrolled it, then drew the rod components from their pockets one by one as she assembled it. Her own rod paled in comparison to Rachel's. Gorgeous deep blue carbon blanks with a silver band edging the wrap at each section's end, the rod was so much more sensitive and responsive than her own. Someday, she'd allow herself to spend the money on a custom fly rod. In the meantime, she didn't mind borrowing one.

She attached the reel and threaded the line, then clipped a small box of flies and a pair of forceps onto the rings on the wader belt. She locked the car, secured her keys on a carabiner clip, then made her way down to the riverbank.

She'd come to the Lower Provo River, a wide spot where the river ran surprisingly smooth, given what Rachel had told her about the cold, wet spring delaying the mountain runoff. The Upper Provo, her preferred fly fishing river, was still running hard, turbulent and filled with debris from the melting snow. But here, below the second of two reservoirs on the river, the water flowed just right.

It didn't matter if she caught anything today. It was the experience of fishing she came for, not the victory of the catch. Besides, between her long work hours and the time she devoted to being a good fiancée to Peter, she hadn't spent time on a river in a couple of years. It would probably take a while before she smoothed out her casting rhythm.

She stepped into the water, carefully selecting a place to plant her feet so she could work a good section of the river. She fumbled several casts, her line failing to pay out properly, plopping into the water. Sheesh, had she forgotten everything Dad taught her? This used to be a rhythm she felt in her soul, pulsing in time with her heartbeat. She tried again. Finally, she drew a deep, steadying breath, pushed aside the frustration and the lack of confidence, and smoothly drew the rod back, forward, back, forward again. There. A proper four-beat cast, and all was right with the world. She'd found her way back as if she'd never been lost.

As she danced the fly over the water, settling for a bit before lifting off again, she let her thoughts drift. A delivery had come that morning before she left the house. Roses, from Peter, and a note directing her to check her email, where he explained what drove him to send her flowers. He'd found a job in Boston and his boyfriend was moving with him. Her leaving gave him the shove he needed to try to be honest with himself.

She was genuinely happy for him. Still, if she thought about it too much, it left her feeling stupid, naïve, and more than a little used. The brain understood. The emotions, the pride, the longing to not be alone, didn't.

A shimmer of color flashed through the water where her fly bobbed on the water, and then the fly vanished, line flying out as the fish zipped away. She lifted the rod against the tug of the fish, pulling the line with her other hand. She worked the fish gently toward her. Gorgeous dark spots covered the fish's back and sides: a lovely brown trout. She let the line slack a bit, working with the fish until it flipped itself off the barbless hook and swam free. She always felt better when the fish left the hook on their own, avoiding any potential damage she might do if she had to handle them to return them to freedom.

Andri looked to the left as a fellow fisher approached along the bank. He was an older man, brown hair shot with gray, tanned face lined with age and likely a whole lot of time spent outdoors. His fishing vest hung open over a pot belly and khaki waders. "That was a good lookin' trout there."

She smiled. "First bite of the day, can't complain."

"If you're working upstream, there's a real nice hole 'bout a hundred yards up, on the far side. At least one big boy in there. He's too wily for my flies, though. Maybe you'll have better luck."

She thanked him and he lifted a hand in farewell as he made his way downstream. She fished along several hundred yards of the river through the afternoon, having no better luck with the fat rainbow the older fisherman had mentioned than he had. Still, it was always worth trying. She crossed paths with a couple of other fishers, but on both occasions, they each merely nodded at the other.

The solitude generated peace. The rich, living scent of the river, the soft rustle of leaves and branches when the breeze kicked up, the twitter of birds, the sun's heat on her skin all worked to set her mind free.

She'd come to Utah with a lot to sort out, and as she sifted through her options, she realized she was content here. She'd enjoyed living in Salt Lake during college. She'd never been a fan of intense heat and she loved having seasons. The only thing pulling her back to Phoenix was her mother. Just because Ma lived there didn't mean she had to.

She really didn't want to go back. She knew some people but she hadn't really engaged with anyone locally. Peter had provided much of her Phoenix social circle. Her true friends were spread all over the country, staying in touch online. Except now that she was here, spending time with Rachel, she realized how much she'd missed having girl time. Going out with some of Rachel's friends the other night was great fun, too.

It was time to start poking around for job leads, which shouldn't be too bad. The state was a tech magnet, perfect for someone with her skill set. She had enough money in savings to get an apartment and start creating some stability while looking for work. She toyed with the details of such a move as she wrapped up fishing and drove back to Rachel's. This would be great. She could breathe here.

Her breath vanished when she pulled onto Rachel's street and found Travis Holt's black pickup in the driveway next to the work van.

Chapter Five

Andri pulled into the driveway behind Rachel's van. Maybe it wasn't his truck. There had to be dozens of black pickups in the Park City area, right? Oh, who was she kidding. He was here, and she was in no condition to face him. Mentally, she'd have time to square her thoughts away before she walked in the house, but physically? A glance in the rearview mirror confirmed what a toll the day took on her appearance.

Her ponytailed hair was windblown, strands waving and curling all over after working their way free of the band. She wore no makeup at all, and the shine on her skin screamed for powder. A faded, bleach-spotted green T-shirt and denim shorts completed her casual day look, but at least she wasn't wearing her waders. She'd actually shaved her legs this morning, her only saving grace.

She sighed. Well, if he wasn't scared off already, this would do it. That was a good thing. Major life changes and starting a relationship should probably be mutually exclusive endeavors. Besides, he was not a candidate, she reminded herself. Too much baggage wrapped up in an irresistible package. Nothing but trouble. Ugh. Why was he here?

When she walked in the house, she heard voices in the family room. She followed the sound and found Ian and Travis talking on the couch, a half-empty pitcher of iced tea on the coffee table beside the bouquet of roses she'd left there.

Ian grinned at her. "How was fishing, Andri?"

"Good." She shifted her gaze, warmth spreading through her when eyes the blue of a winter sky met hers. Heaven help her, Travis was handsome, dressed in a creamy button-down shirt and navy trousers.

Surprise crossed his face. "What, you fish?"

Oh-ho, she'd caught his attention without even trying. That kind of made up for the fact she looked a mess. A shiver of delight rippled along her spine. "Fly fish, yeah. Had to go a ways to find good conditions, but a bad day fishing is still better than a good day at work."

"True." He looked impressed. "I did not see that coming."

"I'm full of surprises. Speaking of which, why are you here?"

His lips curled into a sexy smile. "My presence was requested for dinner."

Rachel entered the room from the kitchen, red hair braided in tails on either side of her neck. "Oh good, you're home."

The grin slowly spread across Rachel's face as everything clicked together in Andri's head. Rachel was playing matchmaker. *Terrific.* She fixed Rachel with the most dagger-filled glare she could manage, then glanced at Travis.

He looked back and forth between her and Rachel, his smile dimming slightly, eyes shadowing. "Hey, Andri, I can take off if this is a problem."

She instantly switched to damage control mode, unwilling to hurt his feelings no matter how much she'd like to strangle her friend. She smiled at him. "No, it's fine, but I would have loved five minutes to shower before I ran into you. A girl has to preserve some illusions, like that she always looks halfway decent."

His appreciative gaze dragged over her. "Oh, I don't know. There's something very attractive about a woman who's all windblown from fishing."

She ignored the hot flash bursting over her skin, a little mortified over how easily his soft tone made her pulse bounce. "Yeah? I smell like the river, too, if that floats your boat. I'm going to hop in the shower."

She beat a hasty retreat upstairs, grabbed her robe out of her room, and locked herself in the bathroom. Okay, clearly Rachel was bent on getting her together with Travis. She stripped and stepped into the shower flow. She trusted Rachel's judgment, and she'd known the man forever, so Andri turned the idea over again for a fresh look.

If she was planning to stay here, assuming she could find a job, then maybe she should continue seeing him. He didn't want anything heavy, right? That was a point in his favor. Plus, she'd have someone to do things with until she got established and could meet new people. She'd probably see him frequently anyway when hanging out with Rachel. Maybe they could at least be friends. Yes, that's it. Develop a friendship. Maybe with a few benefits on the side. Dating buddies. Nothing serious.

Andri endured a cooler than normal shower, for the sake of her sanity, and made her way to the kitchen fifteen minutes later. An ivory headband held the damp hair off her face, and she smoothed the tail of her pink cotton shirt over her clean black shorts as she came down the stairs. She wondered if she imagined Travis's double-take when he looked up from the cutting board on the counter, where he stood chopping lettuce for a salad.

"I see Rachel put you to work," she said, taking the plates from Rachel as she passed her and placing them on the table.

He smiled. "Actually, Ian started dinner, and I'm not one for letting another man suffer in the kitchen by himself."

Rachel snorted. "Andri, don't listen to him. He loves to cook."

"Guilty as charged." Travis chuckled, turning his attention back to his vegetables. The man liked her outdoorsy side *and* knew how to cook? Andri stifled a sigh. She'd given an inch on being willing to maybe try dating, but she'd fall a freaking mile if she wasn't careful.

The door leading in from the back deck opened and Ian leaned in, the scent of sizzling beef from the gas grill wafting into the house with him. "Andri, how do you want your steak?"

"Rare enough that a good vet can still save it."

Ian laughed and Travis nodded approval. "Woman after my own heart."

Andri set the last plate and left Rachel to distribute utensils and glasses. She passed by Travis and swiped a freshly cut tomato wedge from his cutting board. He growled at her, then added the tomatoes, cucumber slices and chopped mushrooms to the salad bowl with long, dexterous fingers she ached to have against her skin. Nothing major, really. Just to hold her hand. That's all. "My, my you are a domestic soul, Mr. Holt."

He shot her a dark look, the effect ruined by the humor in his eyes. "Hey, I'm just doing whatever I can to move things along, since I'm hungry. Purely self-preservation."

She reached for a snappy reply, but couldn't find one. The slow, sexy grin spreading across his lips mesmerized her. A flicker of heat sparked deep inside her, and she mentally shook herself, trying to tamp it down. Luckily, Ian saved her, pushing the door open, balancing a platter of sizzling steaks.

Travis surprised her when he set the salad bowl on the table, then stepped over and held her chair as she sat next to Rachel. He settled across the table from her.

Conversation picked up easily between the four of them, the way words should flow with ease at a family table. Of course, in her family, words frequently overflowed, as likely into loud arguments as into shrieks of laughter, especially when visiting extended family. Either way, tears regularly followed. Here, in Rachel's home, there didn't seem to be much arguing, but there was always plenty of warmth and kindness, with meals offering nourishment in the form of emotional support as well as food.

Travis fit here, a testament to how long he'd known Rachel's family. He poured himself another glass of iced tea.

The conversation rolled along, with each of them contributing details of their day. When Ian explained the curriculum of the training camp he was heading to in Lake Placid, New York, in a few days, Andri found her focus shifting repeatedly to Travis. She took in the little details of his appearance, like the pinky finger on his right hand that looked a little crooked and didn't seem to bend quite right. When had he broken it?

She glanced at his tanned, clean-shaven face when he wasn't looking at her, surreptitiously studying his strong features. She could be friends with him. Probably. The twisting heat in her belly reminded her just how much she wanted to kiss him again. What were the chances that she could do that, spend time kissing him and still keep herself from absorbing the pain she knew lurked inside him? If she could just keep her heart from engaging…

She rose, taking her plate to the sink. The sudden silence caught her attention and as she mentally backtracked, she realized she'd exited a spirited conversation without warning.

Three pairs of eyes studied her as she turned around. "Um, great steak, Ian. Sorry, don't mind me. I'm just going to step out and get some air." She smiled as brightly as she could, then escaped through the back door.

She dropped onto the porch swing, propped her elbow on the wood arm, leaned her head against her hand. Andri closed her eyes and drew a deep breath, letting the cool pine-scented air flow through her, easing her pounding heart. Soon, she heard the back door open, and footsteps crossing the deck. A floorboard in the middle of the deck creaked when stepped on. She recalled it being the same when she spent time here during college. Rachel's dad must have never gotten around to fixing it before he retired and moved to Florida.

"Mind if I join you?"

Her eyes flew open at the low, smooth sound of Travis's voice. "Be my guest."

Travis lowered himself beside her, seeming careful not to touch her. He pushed off slightly with his feet, putting the swing into gentle motion. "It's nice out here. I always liked this swing."

"Did you have one at your home, growing up?"

He shook his head. "Uh, no. Not my mother's style. She's an elegant woman. Something this quaint wouldn't work with her decorating schemes. She has an amazing garden, though. She lets the plants do as they will. It's as wild and loose as she gets."

"She sounds like an interesting woman, but I think she missed out. Every house should have a porch swing."

"Did you, growing up?"

"Oh, yeah. We had a tiny front porch, just big enough for a swing beside the door. It was always one of my favorite spots. I did more serious thinking, and more daydreaming, there than anywhere else."

His voice softened. "And which are you doing now?"

Andri turned her head and found Travis studying her, concern shadowing his eyes in the golden evening light. "Neither. I've been thinking all day. Time for a break."

He nudged her foot with his own when he gave the swing another push, but she couldn't be sure if he'd touched her intentionally or not. "So what were you thinking about all day while playing with the fish?"

The question jolted her a bit, signaling a more serious turn in the conversation. "Life."

"Major subject. Come to any earth-shattering conclusions?"

"Yeah. I'm not going back to Phoenix. I'm going to settle here in Utah, assuming the job hunt is successful."

"Oh, really?" He looked a little stunned, then smiled at her in that slow, sexy way that made her stomach flip.

"Really. And, you know, if I'm going to stay, I could use a social circle. Want to be my friend?"

His expression brightened. "Sure."

That was easier than she'd expected. "Good. I'll need help moving."

Travis groaned. "Figures. There's always a catch to the friend thing."

"What are friends for?"

He appraised her for a moment. "Here's a topic for you, friend. Rachel said the roses inside were from your ex."

She sobered. Still a little twinge of inadequacy, but she'd gone a long way in getting it out of her system today. "Yeah. They were to say thank you. Things are working out for him. His life is going in a far better direction since I backed out of his little scheme. I'm really happy for him."

He shook his head, chuckled softly. "I think you're the only woman I've ever known who would say such a thing, given the situation. God knows I can't be that charitable about my ex."

"Tell me about her." The words came out before she could stop them, followed by a moment of sheer panic. Did she really want to know? Especially if that was the source of the misery locked inside him. Maybe it wasn't too late to retract the question.

Travis looked at her for a moment, an edge of old pain etched in his expression as he seemed to weigh his words. Finally, he drew a deep breath and slowly released it. "I met Melody at a party, a barbecue a friend of a friend held, the summer after I finished my MBA program. I'd dated when I had time, but suddenly I was out of school, just working, and I really had the time to pursue a relationship. She was someone new. I thought she was hot and she found me interesting, for whatever reason. I think that was the biggest appeal. She came on strong, and I was only too happy to go along for the ride."

Okay, so far so good. Maybe this wasn't too deep a subject. Plus, friends knew things about each other. She wasn't getting too close to him yet. "When did you get married?"

Travis ran his fingers down the swing chain, the thick metal links stark against the red and pink splashes of sunset coloring the clouds over the mountains. "I asked her to marry me just before Christmas, trying to be perfectly romantic, you know? To make it even more disgustingly sweet, we married on Valentine's Day."

"That's one way to ruin a holiday. Happened to me, too. Peter and I got engaged on Valentine's Day."

He cracked a smile. "So you're with me on boycotting the holiday."

"Oh, yes." She suddenly pictured herself and Travis next Valentine's Day, gleefully burning sappy greeting cards, then challenging each other on some video game filled with over-the-top violence and lots of blood. *Perfect.*

"The first year was okay. After that, we fought all the time. Things fell apart." He shifted beside her, and she felt the gradual change in his mood as he spoke. "Nothing major was wrong, you know, but everything was wrong at the same time. Next thing you know, it's 'irreconcilable differences' in legal papers. After we divorced, she moved to California. I haven't seen or heard from her since. I'm sure she's equally grateful for that."

There was more. She could see the tension in the way he held himself, in his fingers drumming against his thighs. His jaw tightened and in that moment, he seemed a million miles away.

She couldn't stop herself, needing to bring him back from the obviously painful place he'd gone. She laid a hand on his forearm. The contact sparked in a bolt of light zipping across her skin.

He covered her hand with his, cascading warmth through her. Then his gaze locked onto hers and her breath caught. The storm clouds swirling behind the dark blue before the gates slammed shut pained her.

His expression cleared and he squeezed her hand. She squeezed back, her inherent need to shoulder his burdens ebbing. "Well, aren't we a pair of walking relationship disasters?"

He shrugged. "Not exactly walking. Swinging, at the moment."

She giggled and he laughed with her, further lightening the load on her heart. She could do this. She could manage her responses to his pain, avoid sacrificing herself on the altar of the darkness locked up inside him. Avoid turning into her dad.

They sat in silence for a moment, watching the brilliance of the sky fade until a strong breeze kicked up from behind them. Tendrils of her hair lifted, blowing across his shoulder and into her face. She turned toward him as he reached up with his free hand. He smoothed her hair away from her face, scooping a handful of wavy strands into his palm and caressing it with his thumb.

Andri swallowed hard, her heart tripping at the gentle pressure of his hand in her hair.

He looked at the strands for a moment. "Your hair is so pretty," he said softly, a huskiness edging his words. His gaze flicked up to hers, the deep blue even darker in the growing twilight. His focus dropped to her mouth and she didn't dare breathe as he tucked her hair back over her shoulder. His fingertips traced along her neck, where he surely saw her pulse beating like a hummingbird's wings. Up, to her jaw, to her chin.

She gasped as he leaned down, his fingers nudging her face up, his warm breath against her lips. *Yes, oh, yes.*

A staccato burst of noise from the neighboring yard jolted her and she pulled back as he threw a sharp glare next door. "Firecrackers."

Andri concentrated on calming her pulse, relishing the connection of his hand holding hers, but mourning the kiss she'd lost. "I recall those being illegal."

"Yep. Sounds like someone made a trip to Evanston already to prep for the Fourth. As long as they don't shoot off any aerials, they probably won't get caught." His gaze returned to hers, but the heat, the moment they'd nearly had, was gone.

She should be grateful. Wouldn't this all go much smoother if they stayed in the friend zone for a while before playing with the potential benefits?

Travis gave her hand another gentle squeeze, then released her. He set his feet against the floorboards, stopping the swing, and stood. "I'd better go. I have some bids to look over tonight."

She rose to walk him out. "Taking work home with you?"

He stretched, grimacing as if a muscle twinged when he moved. "It's what I get for spending so much time out on site lately. Have to pay the price eventually."

Travis opened the door and ushered her through into the kitchen. Rachel had apparently cleaned up without their help. Andri felt a tiny prick of guilt at that, but hey, this whole evening had been Rach's idea, so perhaps cleaning was her just punishment.

Andri followed him down the entry hall to the front door. Craving one last connection before he left, she brushed her fingertips across the back of his hand.

A thrill jogged her heart when he grabbed her fingers and gave them a light squeeze before stepping through the doorway.

He turned back to face her. "Tell Rach thanks for dinner. I owe her one."

"You do?"

"Yeah. She gave me a chance to talk to you. Do you think you'll answer my texts now?"

She enjoyed the tingle of excitement for two seconds before pushing it away. "I might even answer your calls. Goodnight, Travis."

He smiled, just enough to crease his dimples. "Goodnight."

She closed the door, then watched him through the sidelight as he walked to his truck, illuminated by the solar pathway lights. He looked so good, his shoulders just the right amount of broad, his hips just the right amount of narrow. He had a really great butt. And his taste...her mind jumped back to that evening in his truck, wrapped in his arms. She couldn't help craving more. She dropped the curtain and pressed her forehead against the heavy wood door, still warm from the heat of the day.

He would haunt her dreams tonight. She knew it, and there wasn't a single thing she could do to prevent it.

Andri turned away from the door and nearly leapt out of her skin when the doorbell rang. When she opened the door again, Travis stood there, a sheepish grin on his face.

Her heart kicked into high gear again as she hoped for one crazy moment that he'd decided to kiss her again before he left. "Hi. Welcome back."

He shook his head. "It's just for a minute. I wanted to ask you—my mother holds an annual fundraiser for the children's hospital. It's coming up at the end of July. If you're planning on sticking around, would you like to go with me?"

Bubbles of joy rose inside her, spreading a glow likely visible a mile away. "I'd love to."

He returned her smile. "Thanks. It's black tie, but it's generally an enjoyable event."

Wow, a big deal. That meant shopping. Serious Shopping, with a capital S, not easy shopping at one of the many cheapish big box options she favored. Not her favorite activity, mainly because her taste didn't always coincide with what stores had to offer, but she'd make the effort. "I'm game."

"I hoped you would be. Night, Andri."

Chapter Six

Making life decisions set Andri in motion. Saturday morning, she begged off the waterskiing trip with Rachel and several of her friends so she'd have time to get her life in order. She made arrangements for a moving company to ship her belongings from her storage unit in Phoenix to Rachel's garage, since she adamantly vetoed the idea of Andri getting a local storage unit. Who knew where she'd find an apartment she liked, but at least her belongings would be here and ready to move when she did get a place.

Rachel wasn't agreeable on the idea of apartment hunting, either. She didn't see why Andri couldn't just go from guest to roommate and stay with her. Andri craved her own space and tended to get a little stir-crazy when she didn't have it. She thought it stemmed from growing up in a contentious family in an itty-bitty house. There was never room to escape. Rachel, on the other hand, had grown up in this roomy farmhouse. It was obvious how much she loved the place, given that she'd bought it from her parents. She envied her friend's ridiculously high level of happy, settled, comfortable living.

She sent emails to contacts, starting her job hunt. Finally, when she couldn't find an excuse to put it off any longer, she sat down to call her mother. The dread weighed her down.

She'd strung her mother along since she'd come to Utah, saying only that she'd be home soon. Time to tell her what she'd decided to do. She gritted her teeth and tapped Ma's name in her contact list.

As soon as she heard Andri's voice, her mother started chattering about all the minute details of her life since she'd last talked to her a couple of days ago. Andri listened, inserting all the right comments along the way so Ma would know she'd been paying attention.

"What are you doing today, Andromeda?"

Confrontations with Ma were inevitable but no matter how old she got, she never managed to shake the feeling of being ten years old, curled in a ball in the corner of her room, trying to shrink down to nothing while her mother screamed at her. Apprehension clamped around her stomach. Ma wasn't going to be happy. "I've made some decisions."

"Oh? Am I going to like them?" Her tone sounded even, but that was part of the way she tricked everyone. There was no warning, just the explosion.

"Probably not. I'm staying in Utah. In fact, I need you to meet the movers at my storage unit with the key on Monday afternoon so they can collect everything."

She started muttering in Greek. Oh, that was never good.

"Ma, this is a good thing for me. After things ended with Peter—"

"Yes, Peter, that reminds me. I heard this morning from his sister that he's moving to Boston. You broke his heart and now we lose a strong member of the community here. It's terrible!"

Andri held her tongue with monumental effort. Ma would never understand because she couldn't explain, not if she wanted to protect Peter. She'd given up trying to please her mother a long time ago, so it really didn't matter if she blamed her for failing to get married. "He's starting over, and so am I."

More muttering. "I should come to you, keep an eye on you."

"Ugh, Ma, really. I'll be thirty this year. I'm a big girl."

"Yes, you are. I know you're all grown up, believe me. I had two children old enough to be in school by the time I was thirty, and—"

Andri cut her off before she could fully launch into a tirade. "Yes, Ma. Even if I wasn't an adult, and required supervision, I wouldn't want to drag you out of Phoenix. I know how much you love it."

"Yes. This is my home, my favorite place since leaving Greece. I don't wish to leave it, but, God knows, children always come first for a mother."

The irony dripped off her mother's words, though she was oblivious to it. Ma always remembered things differently than she and Dmitri did. "Ma, no. You don't need to leave. Please, *Manoula*, I'll be fine, I promise. Don't worry. This will be good for me."

A long silence made her glance at the phone, to be sure the call hadn't disconnected. Finally, her mother sighed. "It's a good community in Salt Lake. Very strong. If I had to leave Phoenix, I would choose to come there to be with our people. Get involved with the community, Andri. You're too much like your father. And, by God, promise me you'll go to church. Maybe the saints will take pity on you and show you the path to another decent man. Maybe this time you won't walk away."

Her words yanked a vision of Travis into her head. Definitely not what her mother had in mind for her, unless his family tree had at least one Greek root in there somewhere. But, no. She'd already made that decision. Friends only, maybe some benefits on the side, but definitely friends. "I promise I'll make it to church, Ma."

"And look for a husband."

"Love you, Ma. Gotta run, busy day, lots to do." Andri slumped in her chair, dropping the phone on the side table. That had gone well, much better than she'd expected. Ma had always tended to be temperamental, but now that she was sober, it was easier to catch her on a good day, when the muttering and sighing wouldn't necessarily escalate into screaming and throwing things. Today, she'd gotten lucky. Maybe that was a sign that she was doing the right thing.

Her phone chimed as a text came in. She picked it up, a shiver of delight coursing down her spine as she checked the name on the text.

Travis: *Hey there. Busy?*

She typed a response. *Not really. Any ideas on a nice apartment complex for me?*

A moment later, the phone chimed.

Travis: *Can recommend a few. Wanna check em out & get dinner?*

She grinned. *Yes. Pick me up or should I meet you?*

Travis: *I'm at home. Be there in a bit.*

She sat on the front porch steps, reading email on her phone until Travis pulled into the driveway. He surprised her by climbing out of the truck and walking with her to the passenger door, opening it and handing her up into the truck. His manners were impeccable, even when they were being totally casual and just friends.

"Is it safe to assume you want to be down in the valley? Or, up here where the living is great but the commute's a pain in the ass?" he asked as they drove toward the canyon interstate.

"If I manage to find work in Park City or Heber, I can always move, but I think chances are higher I'll end up somewhere along the Wasatch Front."

He glanced at her. "So, centrally located for now."

"That's what I was thinking."

He grinned. "I think I know just the place. Well, a couple of them in the same general area. Nice, safe, lots of shopping and restaurants nearby, good freeway access."

She shifted in her seat to face him. "Perfect. You read my mind."

"I try. Need to stop by the office first for a minute, if that's okay."

"Sure." That could be interesting. She learned a lot about people from observing their workspace. Their personalities, what they loved, a lot of their idiosyncrasies showed up on cubicle walls, desks, and computer desktops.

Travis's gaze flicked to meet hers, then back to the road. "How's your day been?"

"Busy. Let's see." She ticked items on her fingers. "I have movers arriving Tuesday afternoon with my storage unit worth of belongings. Got the job search underway. And for that added bit of extra excitement, I talked to my mother."

His brows lifted and he shot her a curious look. "Sounds like things are tense there."

Tense? Oh, yeah. "It's complicated. I love my mother, I do, and she can be really wonderful sometimes. But she's opinionated and a bit on the volatile side. She's clinging harder to heritage and tradition the older she gets, so I'm never sure how she's going to react to things. Today she was in a good mood, so I survived telling her I'm staying in Utah."

He chuckled. "Parents. What are you going to do with them?"

"Exactly. I had to promise I'd get involved with the Greek community here. We have such a small family in this country that the community has always been the replacement for cousins. I think she's afraid all the ethnicity will drain out of me if I'm not surrounded by people who can pour more in."

"Sounds like my dad and his emphasis on family ties. We've had huge gatherings with aunts and uncles and cousins several times a year since I was a kid, and attendance is mandatory. Good thing I like most of my cousins."

"How big are these gatherings?"

"The Miceli side of the family, my mother's, is fairly small, but on the Holt side, I have three aunts, four uncles, their spouses, thirty-six cousins, most of whom are married now. And then there's the herd of children, my second-cousins. We're flirting with twenty of those already, and it's just going to get worse as we get older."

Andri's mouth dropped. "Are you sure you're not Greek? Sounds like our trips to see Ma's family in Corfu."

"It's a madhouse. You'd think the craziness would get to my dad and he wouldn't want to host family parties anymore, but I can't even get him to slow down at work, let alone unwind on the family thing." He paused, and a shadow flickered across his face. "I'm worried about him. He hasn't felt very well the last few weeks, but getting him to the doctor is next to impossible."

That sounded familiar, but she certainly wasn't going to say so. No sense inviting trouble. Her father was never fond of going to the doctor, either, and it had ended badly. She wouldn't wish that on anyone else.

When they reached the construction company headquarters, Andri went in with him. The doors opened into a large, airy space, with dark gray stone floors and pale blue walls accented with gray wood and frosted glass tiles. A few doors led off the main room, other offices. A couple of white leather sofas and dark gray chairs offered comfortable seating near a desk. Large flat-screen monitors hung on two walls, and Andri wondered what they might display during business hours. Slideshows of properties the company had built, probably. That's how she would use them.

The rooms were quiet except for the bluesy music coming from one of the offices. Travis set the folders in his hands on the desk in the main room and she followed him to investigate.

A young man at a computer spun around in his seat when they entered his office. Jet black hair brushed his shoulders and swept down to the tip of his nose. He absently brushed it back, exposing a fierce black eye and angry red scrapes across his forehead and cheek.

Travis cursed and crossed the floor, bracing his hands on either side of the young man's head, tilting his face up to the light. "Daniel, what happened?"

Oh, yes. His brother.

He winced when Travis touched his cheekbone. "Got into a fight, what does it look like?" He shrugged off Travis's hands and nodded at her. "Hi. I'm Danny." His hair was darker, but his eyes were the same deep blue, and they shared the same high cheekbones and strong jaw. The stark lines of a black tribal tattoo wound around Danny's bicep, just visible under the edge of his gray t-shirt sleeve.

She waved her fingers at him. "Andri."

Travis crossed his arms over his chest and fixed Danny with a hard stare. "What were you fighting over?"

Danny's expression turned mulish. "What does it matter? It happened. It's over. You should be happy I'm in here on a Saturday working on that plan redraw."

Travis grabbed one of his brother's hands, looking at the smooth knuckles. "You weren't in a fight. You were beaten. What the hell, Dan?"

Andri took a few steps back. This was a conversation between brothers, something she really shouldn't be privy to. Feeling distinctly uncomfortable, she stepped out of the office to give them some measure of privacy. It didn't help, she still heard them talking.

"Who did you owe money to?" Travis asked, a thread of resignation wound through the anger in his voice.

"Just some asshole dealer I used to buy from. I paid him, but he wanted to make sure I wouldn't leave him hanging again."

"How long have you owed him money?"

"It's old debt, from before rehab this last time. I'm clean, I swear to God."

"Danny, you have to be. You can't do this anymore. You're playing with your life." Desperation tinged his words, and made Andri's heart ache, wringing memories from the dark corridors of her mind.

"Zoe, please. You can't keep doing this. You're destroying yourself, you're hurting the kids." Her father's face contorted with anguish, his hands shaking as he reached for Ma. "God, woman, you're breaking my heart."

Ma stormed over to the fireplace, hurling her wineglass into the grate, screaming, "There! Are you happy now?" She threw the empty wine bottle into the fire. "I hate you, Michael! I hate you! I'm tired of you saying I'm a bad mother because I like a glass of wine!"

And that was always the trouble. One glass of wine was all she ever held in her hand. But she refused to count how many times she'd filled that glass.

Andri crossed to the business's main entrance, not wanting to hear the rest of the conversation between the brothers. She recalled Travis's reaction to her questions about his family that night at the Mexican restaurant. The pain in his gaze. He was locked in the same battle her father had waged most of her life. No wonder the hurt in him called to her need to nurture and soothe. She'd spent her formative years watching the same distress fester in her father, unable to help.

She started when she felt a touch on her shoulder.

Travis stood beside her. "Sorry about that. Are you ready to go?"

She nodded and walked with him out to the truck. She brushed her fingers along his as they walked. She couldn't help it. He took her hand, wove his fingers between hers, breaking the connection only to help her into the truck.

She didn't want to touch his stress with the proverbial ten-foot pole, but she had to ask. "Everything okay?"

He smiled, the closed doors behind his eyes shielding the place where he stored the hurt. "Yeah. Let's go have a look at those apartments."

At the second complex he showed her, she fell in love with a quiet second-floor end unit. It wouldn't be ready for her to move in for a couple of weeks, but she didn't mind waiting. The location was ideal, she could have a pet, and the list of amenities thrilled her.

They went out for burgers and then drove back to Rachel's house. Rachel had left a note after waterskiing, reminding her that she'd gone to see a musical at the Capitol Theatre. With Ian out of town, Andri had the house to herself. She held out a hand to Travis when he walked her to the front door. "Want to come in for a bit?"

"Sure." He took her hand and followed her inside. He accepted her offer of soda and met her on the couch when she arrived with a can for each of them.

She settled beside him. "I guess I'd better call the movers Monday morning and reschedule. Maybe I can time it so that they can deliver on the day I get the keys."

"That puts you into July, though. Another month's rent on your storage unit."

"That's true. But it would save you from helping me move from here to the apartment."

He shook his head. "Don't worry about it. I said I'd help and I don't mind. I'll have to call in some friends to help get your furniture up to the second floor, though."

"That would be appreciated. I'm sure I'll owe you something for that."

"A token of thanks would be appropriate."

Andri considered the options for a moment. "Hmm. I'll buy pizza for everyone who shows up to help."

Travis stretched his legs out and settled back into the couch cushions, lacing his fingers behind his head. "That would definitely take care of the guys."

"But not you?"

"No, I'm more expensive." Oh, the way that slow grin of his made her insides go all gooey distracted her to no end.

"Okay. I'll cook you dinner as soon as my place is put together."

He mulled her offer. "Not often a woman cooks for me. I could live with that."

"Great. You'll be my first dinner guest in my new place." She relaxed against the back of the couch and smiled at him. Warmth filled his eyes and he took her hand, tracing his thumb over her knuckles. The motion tingled up her arm, heating her blood.

"Are you serious about adopting a cat?"

She grinned. "Absolutely. I haven't had a pet since I was a kid." A memory surfaced. Spirit, her little mutt, who had shored her up during his fourteen years of life. She really missed him, even now. "I can't guarantee I'll be home enough to take good care of a dog, but cats are pretty self-sufficient. I think it could work out nicely."

He stretched his other arm along the back of the couch, catching a tendril of her hair between his fingers. "My mother wouldn't allow cats in the house because of the shedding. I've always liked them, though."

Andri was a firm believer in the wonderful things pets did for a person, especially children. Her dog was her confidant and comforter, resting patiently in her arms for hours when she hid from Ma's tirades, from the screaming, from the hurtful words that proved the mean girls at school were complete amateurs. "Did you have any pets?"

"I had a hamster. Tiny little thing, a Russian dwarf. I called her Zippy. Danny wanted a dog, but Mother absolutely refused. So he'd beg Uncle Mac to bring his family's golden retriever to the parties."

"I'm guessing that went over well."

"Mother allowed it, but only if Danny cleaned up whatever messes old Sunshine made. He never complained. For him, playing with that dog was worth every moment of picking up after her."

His smile warred with the hint of wistfulness in his voice and the deeper emotions banked behind his gaze. "Hey…I'm sorry you had to be there through my discussion with Dan this afternoon."

She squeezed his fingers. "It's fine. I tried to make myself scarce so it didn't embarrass him too much."

He sat quietly for a moment, staring at her hand in his. "You know, my brother has had problems for a long time now. Dealing with it consumes whole days sometimes."

A dark cloud gathered in her chest, memories of her own experiences 'dealing with it' sifting up from the recesses of her mind. "Drugs?"

Travis winced. "Cocaine. Alcohol. Marijuana. I just thank God that's all. He lost a friend to meth last year. You'd think that alone would convince him to get clean and stay that way, but he manages to convince himself that he's different."

That sounded familiar. "I thought I heard him say he'd been in rehab."

"Twice now. Ninety days this last time. He just got out the end of May." He sighed heavily. "I don't think it helped. He's already had one relapse that I know of."

What did she say to that? "I'm sorry, Travis. I know how painful that must be for you."

He shook his head, then chuckled softly and put on a bit of a smile. "Wow, I really turned this evening into a downer. I apologize."

"Hey, don't worry about it. I enjoy talking to you, no matter what subject comes up." Andri understood the shift he'd made, and the best thing she could do at this point was let it go. He was hurting, but unwilling to voice it, whether in general or because they still didn't know each other very well. She knew how hard it could be to talk about life with an addict, but if he wasn't ready to say more, she couldn't really offer any advice. That would be a surefire way to irritate him.

He yawned, then patted her hand and rose to leave. "I enjoy talking to you too, Andri. I'm short on sleep, though, and a tired brain doesn't always choose the best topics."

She walked him out, pausing at the top of the porch stairs. "Thanks for your help with the apartment hunt. That would have taken me forever on my own."

He leaned down, and her breath caught when he kissed her cheek. "Night, Andri."

She watched him drive away, then went inside and turned on the TV. She flipped through channels, not really paying attention to what flashed on the screen. She and Travis were friends. Period. At this point, even getting into benefits might be going too far, but being more than friends was out of the question.

One addict in her life, albeit a recovered one, was the limit of what she could handle. She hadn't realized until that moment how deep the scars from dealing with her mother all her life ran. She liked Travis a great deal, and she really liked their chemistry. It didn't matter, not after catching a glimpse of how thickly his brother's addiction twined around Travis's life. How could she willingly invite that destructiveness into her life again?

She fervently hoped Danny Holt would recover and go on to have a long, happy life. It broke her heart to see people lose their battles, knowing what it cost those who loved them. But right now, the thought of coping with the strain of another addict was too much.

It shook her, recognizing she was damaged in a way she hadn't noticed before. Tears filled her eyes and she let them fall in silence.

* * * *

Andri stayed busy over the next week, working a few days with Rachel. Her belongings arrived from Arizona, and she felt strangely better having her stuff stacked in the garage. It meant progress, made her decisions feel more real. It also meant her own fishing rod was available, so she and Rachel spent time on the river.

Friday was the Fourth of July, and she and Rachel spent the day at a huge park in Salt Lake. Holt Construction threw an annual picnic for their employees and the subs and their families. She saw Travis off and on throughout the day, but he was busy helping with the food, assisting his dad with running some contests. When he did spend a few moments with her, his happy mood rubbed off on her and she found herself enjoying the day more than she'd anticipated.

That night, under a dark, clear sky, Andri joined Rachel in the middle of a mass of blankets, spread on the lawn for watching the impending fireworks. Kids ran past, waving sparklers as she chose her spot and sat cross-legged. Rachel leaned back to study the sky.

Travis arrived a few moments later, having said goodbye to his parents. She turned to look at him as he stretched out beside her, the warm bit of breeze teasing her with his scent, accented with tones of sunscreen and smoke from the grill. His t-shirt clung to his frame just enough to hint at the muscles that shaped his chest and abs.

She let her gaze slide down over his faded jeans, to the rip in one thigh. She imagined how the lightly-furred skin visible beneath the ragged edges of the denim might feel, jerking her thoughts away before she fell to temptation and touched him. This was supposed to be about friendship, right? She did not need a relationship right now. She did not need a relationship with *him*. Better get her mind elsewhere in a hurry. "How's your dad?"

"Fine. I think he wore himself out today. That three-legged race was a bit much." Travis looked around her and lifted a hand to signal someone. Soon, Andri recognized the lanky form of Danny approaching. He'd arrived late tonight, but apparently sober. So far, it looked like Travis was simply going to be happy his brother had shown up. That was a good place for him to be.

Danny nudged Rachel's legs with his foot. "Make a space, Rach."

"And you'll make it worth my while how?"

He narrowed his eyes at her. "I'll tickle you until you can't breathe if you don't."

Rachel snorted. "Come on, kid, try it. I can still take you, and you know it."

"You wish. I suppose I could ask nicely."

"Suppose you could."

Danny adopted a foot-forward stance and gave a flourished bow. "Dearest Rachel, sweet lady, grand friend, Queen of all that Glows with the Might of Electricity, wouldst thou be so kind as to move thy ass, so that I may occupy the smallest of parcels at thy delicate feet and watch the fireworks that shall surely dim in the face of thy beauty?"

Andri laughed and applauded, glancing at Travis and enjoying the happiness etched on his face.

Rachel laughed and pulled her feet up to make room. "That was laid on a bit thick, Danny-boy."

Danny shrugged and sat. He lay back, cushioning his head on his arm. "Yep. Worked, though."

Andri settled on her back, staring up at the sky, but after a moment, Travis scooted flush beside her and urged her to sit up enough that he could slide his arm beneath her head. Her heart tripped into a pounding beat as she rested against his strong shoulder.

When he tilted his head to touch hers, the throbbing of her pulse intensified. It had been so long since someone set off her desire, and it was all she could do not to squeeze her thighs together in response. Clearly, it didn't matter to her hormones what her brain understood about their friendship. He wasn't flirting with her, and heaven knew she didn't want him to, but it sure felt good to have him close.

"Comfortable?" he asked, his breath warm against her cheek.

"Very." No, she was actually getting a little achy, but that wasn't something she needed to share.

"Hmm. Good."

The first firework shell boomed and burst into a thousand points of blue and red light, and as if on cue, Travis, Rachel, and Danny all said, "Ooooooh." They followed the next burst with "Ahhhhhh."

Andri giggled. "You three have done this before."

Travis chuckled and she felt it vibrate through his chest. "Oh, yeah. Wait'll we get to the end. Gotta make a big deal out of the grand finale."

She joined in with the oohs and ahhs after that, trying to ignore the flare of heat in her belly every time he shifted beside her. They were friends. Friends who could enjoy a holiday together and not get any deeper.

Chapter Seven

Travis pulled into the driveway at his parents' house the following Wednesday afternoon, fighting a yawn. Everything had been fine for days, but last night, out of the blue, he'd dreamed about Jacob. Dark, distorted images, twisted sounds. His brother's face, his expression so desolate and unreachable. Screaming until his throat burned. Fighting as hard as he could, but losing…failing… It hung in his mind, creating a haze he couldn't shake for the rest of the day.

He'd considered catching a nap in the office, but with his luck, that would be proclaiming open season on his brain for whatever part of his subconscious enjoyed filling his dreams with the past.

His mother was playing the piano when he walked in past the open entry of the music room. He waved but she merely nodded at him and continued playing. He went into his dad's office, but he wasn't there. Travis found the plans he'd come for and gathered them under his arm, then made a quick trip through the house to find his dad.

Ready to give up, he finally spotted him in the backyard. Travis made his way outside, across the expanse of deep green lawn to the edge of his mother's wild garden. There, Terrence stood on an overgrown path, touching the petals of a row of black hollyhocks, on a stalk as tall as he was.

Feeling strangely like he was interrupting a moment of deep communion between man and nature, Travis said, "Hey, Dad."

Terrence turned, his smile a little wistful. "It looks like you found what you needed."

"Yeah, thanks." Travis watched him approach, his palms brushing various plants as he exited the overgrown craziness that his mother had let take over a good third of the yard. He'd never really understood Mother's unruly garden, but it was their property. If Dad didn't care, then she could do whatever she wanted with it.

He gave his dad a hug. "How are you feeling, now that you've had a couple of days off?"

"Oh, I'm fine," Terrence said, and some of Travis's tension unwound. "The congestion in my chest cleared right up. I think I finally shook that cold this time. Come on, I'll walk you out."

Travis's relief over his dad's improved health put him in a better mood. One that took a nosedive half an hour later when he walked back into the office and saw the distinct disapproval on his office manager's face as she hung up the phone. "What's going on, Peggy?"

"I've rescheduled three of Daniel's appointments today, and the one I just got off the phone with was very unhappy about the change."

Not again. His gut knotted. "Did you talk to him?"

She slipped her glasses off and cleaned the lenses on the end of her purple blouse. "Yes."

"High?"

"Maybe. Definitely hung over."

Travis muttered a curse under his breath, but Peggy caught it anyway. She shook her head. "I know, hon, I know."

He left the plans he'd retrieved at Peggy's desk for the sub who'd need them in the morning. He spent the next few hours wrapping up the rest of the day's duties in a cold funk. What was it going to take to fix Danny? If someone would just give him something concrete he could do to clean up his brother once and for all, he'd sacrifice everything he had to make it happen.

At five-thirty, a calendar reminder beeped from his phone. Damn. He was supposed to see a play with Andri tonight. He was less than pleasant company, too tired and frustrated to enjoy any kind of activity. He thought about cancelling, but he didn't want to let her down. He washed up quickly and put on a fresh shirt before heading off to pick her up.

* * * *

Andri leaned against the porch railing at Rachel's house, waiting for Travis to take her to a play. She grinned when he pulled into the driveway and got out of his truck, looking yummy in a gray shirt and black pants. A little zing of electricity pinged around inside her, until his tired smile and shadowed eyes grabbed her attention. His day had obviously worn him out. *Aww, poor guy.*

He took her hand as she joined him at the bottom of the steps. "Long day at the office?" she asked.

He shrugged. "Nah, I've had worse." He walked her around to the truck's passenger door and opened it for her.

She paused and squeezed his hand. "Travis, we don't have to go if you're tired."

Travis smiled at her, and it looked genuine. "I know."

He was thoroughly pleasant, conversing with her on the drive to the playhouse. But she'd seen him physically tired before, and there was more to his underlying mood than a simple lack of sleep or hours of hard work. Something was definitely off with him. His gaze was walled off more than usual, and his step seemed heavier up the steps to the theater.

When the play proved to be bland and boring, she suggested they leave at intermission. The relief in his expression was undeniable. On the drive back to the house, she wanted to ask him what was wrong, but he gave no indication that he was willing to discuss what weighed on him.

Travis accepted her invitation to come in for a while once they returned to Rachel's house. He turned on the game system while she retrieved iced tea, but whatever distracted him kept him from driving his souped up game car well enough to beat her. That was a first. Racing games were not her strong point.

Finally, he set the controller on the coffee table and groaned, running a hand over his face with a grimace. "I'm sorry, Andri. I'm lousy company. I should call it a night."

Andri gently rubbed his shoulder. "Hey, we all have our off days. What's going on?"

"It's been one of those roller-coaster days, but it took a bad drop toward the end."

"Is your dad still sick?"

He turned toward her. "No, he's feeling great for a change." He reached over and smoothed a stray lock of hair over her shoulder with the rest, his touch sending warmth curling down her torso. "Danny missed work today. Peggy said he sounded hung over, but I couldn't confirm for myself because he didn't answer my calls."

His brother would have been her next guess for the source of his mood. "That's not good."

He sighed. "No, it isn't."

Part of her cried out a warning in the back of her mind that she was about to step into butting-in territory, but she ignored it and dove into the thing she'd thought about since observing the way he and his brother interacted. "Travis, have you ever talked to anyone about Danny?"

"Of course, when he's gone into rehab, I've been there for the initial visit."

"No, that's not what I mean." She knew she had to put this delicately. "Have you talked to someone about him, for yourself? About the strain his addiction puts on you."

His brow furrowed, confusion in his eyes. "Why would I? I mean, yeah, obviously there is some stress in dealing with all of his crap. But he's my brother. He's worth it."

"Of course he's worth it, Travis, that's not what I'm saying." She sighed, knowing she'd gone too far to back up now. "Do you recognize that shouldering the weight of his problems is unhealthy for you? I know you're giving it everything you have, trying to help him and heal him, but…you can't force him to be fixed. You can't save him from himself."

His gaze darkened and he released her hand. "Danny needs my help. He can't do it on his own."

She saw the storm coming, the defensiveness building in his eyes, but she'd come this far. Might as well finish. He needed to hear it, even if he hated her for it. "Ultimately he'll make his own choices, and if he decides not to help himself, and you don't get out of the way, you'll end up a casualty of his choices."

Travis sat up, his gaze frosting into a cool glare. "You know, it's easy to be an armchair quarterback, Andri, but you don't have *any* idea what it's like to be in my shoes. I've been taking care of my brother for a long time now. I know what needs to be done. You don't." His voice was tight, controlled.

She clamped down on the fight rising inside her, resisting the urge to give in to her mother's way of holding a discussion. Screaming wouldn't help. At this point, she doubted he'd listen if she tried to explain her position, that she did know what it was like. She knew the path he was headed down, a path that would disappear in front of him and drop him off the edge of a cliff. But now was clearly not the time to press him. She raised her hands in surrender. "Okay. I'm only trying to help."

He sighed heavily and rubbed his face with one hand. "I know. But I don't need your advice. It would be best if we didn't talk about this subject anymore." He glanced at his phone, checking the time. "I'd better go."

Andri walked him to the door, her heart heavy. He didn't look back as he left. She closed the door behind him and leaned against it. That hadn't gone well. She took a slow, deep breath, trying to release both her frustration and the sting Travis had needled into her skin with his words. She didn't blame him for lashing out. The man was doing everything in his power to save someone he loved. Of course he had reacted with anger and defensiveness when told he was doing it wrong.

Travis wore responsibility like a second skin. He'd never let his brother fall, even if Danny was determined to hit rock bottom. It probably went against everything in Travis to let someone else crash without trying to stop them.

If his need to protect outweighed the instinct for survival, he'd easily be sucked into the riptide. She'd certainly learned that lesson the hard way, and it killed her to see Travis on a collision course with the same harsh schooling. No matter how much his scent and his touch made her insides do funny flips, Travis was her friend, and Andri couldn't let a friend suffer if there was anything at all she could do to help. She hoped she could somehow help Travis learn the lesson looming before him before it blew into him and left him in pieces.

* * * *

Travis worked harder than he ever had over the next several days, dividing his time between the office and assisting crews, driving both brain and body until he collapsed into an exhausted sleep at the end of the day. Heavy sleep kept dreams, whether of his brother or Andri, at bay.

The hard work didn't help him with thoughts of Andri during the day. Little things provided a stream of reminders. A breeze would kick up on the job, and he'd see her in his mind, all cute and windblown from fishing. One afternoon, he pulled cash out of his wallet and a receipt from the last time they had lunch together fell out, making him think about how much she'd loved the butter chicken at that Indian place.

They were just friends, and at the moment she wasn't on his happy list, so why the hell was it so hard to stop thinking about her?

He put in a token appearance at his parents' house when his mother held a dinner party for friends newly returned from a three-year work contract in Japan. Though the fine lines tightening around Mother's mouth spoke her disapproval, she at least didn't verbally chide him for arriving dateless and leaving far too early.

He watched Danny's schedule like a hawk, checking on him in the evenings to make sure everything was going okay. He caught himself thinking about Andri, wondering how the job hunt was going, or when she'd get her apartment keys for sure and be ready to move. He'd promised to help her move, and he'd be there, no matter what. But the frustration with her flippant advice to leave his brother to his own devices still simmered in his chest.

It should be better this way, leaving her friendship behind. He'd searched for something about her that would kill his attraction, and he'd found it. It didn't really help, though. There should have been some relief when he walked away from her. Instead, he had twinges of guilt over hurting her and bursts of desire tugging at him when she crossed his thoughts. Shouldn't he have stopped thinking about her by now?

Travis walked into the office early the next Tuesday and found Rachel pacing in front of his desk. "Hi."

She rounded on him. "You're such an ass."

He hated it when Rachel went on the rampage. "What did I do?"

Rachel planted her feet, hands on her hips, and pinned him with a dark look he knew all too well. Ah. She talked to Andri. "Rach, don't give me that look."

"I racked my brains to see if there was some reason that you might deserve a nugget of my excellent advice. About the only thing I came up with is that I don't recall paying you back for that time at the park the summer after sixth grade when Joe Carlton poured a bucket of sand on my head and you tossed him in the nearest dumpster. So to pay off that debt, listen up. Andri is sweet and genuine and thoughtful and she doesn't usually stick her nose in other people's business. When someone like that offers you advice, maybe you should ask why."

Frustration surged inside him. Naturally Rachel would defend her friend, but he'd known Rachel far longer. Shouldn't she be on his side? "I know why. She was trying to help."

"Yeah, she was." Rachel stepped forward, nearly nose to nose with him, and poked him in the chest to punctuate her words. "Ask. Her. Why."

A sick feeling bloomed in his gut. He'd missed something important, or she wouldn't be busting his balls like this. "Talk to me, Rach."

She flipped him the bird and stalked out of his office. She'd clearly given him all the help she intended to, and with the anger vibrating through her frame, it was probably more help than he deserved.

Damn it all. He utterly despised the embarrassment and regret that followed letting his temper get the best of him. And now he needed to apologize to Andri. He'd obviously wronged her, and his honor would hold his feet to the fire until he made things right.

He dreaded facing Andri again, when his attraction hadn't faded enough. Hell, it hadn't faded at all. He'd spotted a woman walking down the street as he drove yesterday. The only similarity was her long, wavy brown hair, but he thought about how thick and silky Andri's hair was, and he thought about kissing her in his truck, and that little whimper of hers and in no time flat, he was suffering a raging hard-on.

He dropped into the chair behind his desk and drew a deep breath to settle the pounding of his heart. He wiped his damp palms on his pants. He missed her so much, on so many levels. Her company. Her friendship. She was fun to spend time with, and fun had been seriously lacking in his life since he walked out on her.

Dammit, he wanted to spend time with her, kiss her, make love to her— Whoa, he had to back down from that one. That brought him to his sense of reason. He didn't want to get hurt. He didn't want to hurt her. But, of course, he had already, hadn't he?

He had to see her again and try to make things right. If he didn't apologize, he'd never hear the end of it from Rachel. There were other electricians, but few lifelong friends. Rachel asked very little of him over the years, but she had asked this. He refused to let down his sister from another mother.

Unfortunately, work conspired against him, and he didn't get the chance to so much as think about apologizing again until two days later, when a text he'd asked Ian to send hit his phone.

Ian: *Moving day for A tomorrow. Starts @ noon.*

He sent a quick note of thanks back. No matter if they were on speaking terms or not, whether the apology went well or not, he'd be there. His inner Boy Scout would never let him live it down if he failed to show up.

When he arrived at Rachel and Ian's house, the work van had been cleaned out and loaded to the brim. He backed his truck into the driveway. Rachel closed the van doors and raised an eyebrow at him.

"I promised."

Rachel gave him a slight nod of approval. "Good. Get to work."

He lowered the tailgate on the truck, and as he turned toward the garage, he caught sight of Andri through the living room window. She was on the phone, pacing, and by the stressed expression on her face, it wasn't a good conversation. His heart twinged a little at the sight of her. She'd upset him, but that didn't mean he liked seeing her distressed.

He and Ian loaded a floral print sofa and a disassembled platform bed into his truck before Andri came out of the house, twisting her hair into a ponytail. Her eyes were tinged with red, and the strength of the instant rage to punish whoever made her cry shocked him.

She glanced up at him and managed a weak smile, merely a shadow of the one that had captured him the first day. "You didn't have to do this."

"Yes, I did."

Before he could ask about the phone call, Rachel said, "Maybe you should change your number and not tell your mother."

Andri laughed a little, waving the suggestion away with one hand. "Sometimes I forget that listening to her when she gets on a tear is optional. But if I cut her off too soon, she really gets annoyed, and then I get all sorts of crazy voice mails and she calls to pester Dmitri."

"You can't get a word in edgewise anyway," Rachel said, picking up a smaller box and heading for Andri's car. "Just set the phone down somewhere and leave the room. She can rant all she wants and you don't have to hear it."

Travis didn't get another chance to talk to Andri through the rest of the move, other than asking directions on where she wanted certain things at the apartment. He was a little surprised that the four of them managed to do the move, including getting the heavy, bulky furniture up to the second floor.

Afterward, Andri offered pizza as a reward, but Ian and Rachel begged off, each claiming other plans for the evening. One look at Rachel told Travis it was a lie, but it would give him a chance to make his apology without an audience, and for that, he was grateful.

When the Garrett siblings left, Travis found Andri standing in the open doorway of her apartment. She watched him approach, her expression unreadable as she stood back and waved him in.

He stood in the entry, glanced into the living room. She'd already pulled out her laptop, which sat on a small glass end table, a notebook beside it and sticky notes on the edges of the screen. "Notes for the job hunt?"

"Yes. I'm sorry, I owe you dinner for helping me move, but unless you feel like a Mickey-D's run, then it will have to wait." Her tone was cool, tired, matching the expression in her eyes. She reached up a hand to massage one of her shoulders, and he forced back the flash of desire to rub the kinks out of her muscles for her.

He leaned back against the door. "I didn't stay because you owe me food. I wanted to apologize."

Her brows lifted. "Okay."

"I bit your head off the last time we talked, and it was uncalled for. I know you meant to help."

Andri watched him, clearly waiting for more. Okay, so maybe he did need to offer more than a simple apology.

He shifted and swallowed hard. His ability to walk away from her had fled, so he reached for the words to try to smooth their friendship out. "I could blame it on being stressed out of my damn mind, or being sensitive about my efforts to help Danny, or whatever, but I won't. There's really no excuse for my behavior. I had no right to take anything out on you. I acted like an ass, and I'm really sorry."

She appraised him for a moment, then nodded slowly. "Nicely done."

He couldn't resist her. After an afternoon working near Andri, catching her inviting scent as he moved her belongings, the way the sleeveless blue top and shorts she wore hugged her curves, thoroughly imprinting his brain, his resistance had fled completely. He never wanted to do anything to take her smile away again, and he desperately needed to see it now. He glanced again at the sofa, ignoring the wisp of a dream that popped into his head. A dream where he'd found a number of ways to make her smile, to fill her with pleasure. *Nope. Not going there.* "Mind if we sit?"

Andri waved her fingers at him to follow as she walked over to the sofa. She sat, pulling one leg beneath her. Travis joined her, taking care not to position himself too close. She'd let him off the hook a little too easily, though maybe that was payment for helping with the move. Rachel would have kicked his ass and then called it good. Melody would have left him in the doghouse for weeks.

She pushed her dark, wavy hair back over her shoulder, a movement that filled him with a sharp craving for the silky feel of her hair in his hands, tangling his fingers through the thick strands— Travis jerked his wandering thoughts back to the moment and focused.

Andri said, "Travis, I understand why you went off like you did, but you've owned it, and I appreciate that."

That was it? "So…apology accepted?"

She nodded. "While we're at it, I'll apologize too. Not for what I said, because it needed saying. But I am sorry for the effect it had. I know it hurt you. You already feel awful. I didn't want to add to it."

Her advice had stung, abraded his pride, and undercut everything he'd been working so hard to accomplish with Danny. "You definitely said things I didn't want to hear. But, just because I don't like something doesn't automatically make it wrong."

She tilted her head slightly, her gaze holding his. "I speak from experience, you know."

His confrontation with Rachel burst into his thoughts. *Ask. Her. Why.* The pieces clicked into place. Of course. Why would she tackle a sensitive and difficult subject to give him advice unless she had some experience to back her up? Wow, he really was clueless. "Now that my brain is engaging instead of my emotions, I think I get it. You really do understand, don't you?"

A slight, sad smile crossed her lips. "Yes, I really do."

"Who?"

"My mother. She's an alcoholic."

His angry words came back to him. *You don't have any idea what it's like.* Another thought overlapped the first, the memory of her reddened eyes, her sadness earlier, after talking with her mother. Oh, yeah. She did know what it was like. Damn, he was an ass. "You know what I'm going through."

"The dynamic is different, but yes. My dad did all the heavy lifting as Dmitri and I grew up. My mom was always a bit of a diva, and even now she swings from lively and happy to a screaming, crying terror. It was much, much worse when she drank. Dad protected us from the worst of it. But I spent my whole life watching him try everything to fix her. He argued, he ordered, he bribed, he begged. He tried to sweet-talk her into doing the right thing. He'd threaten to leave her until she clung to his leg and begged him to stay."

As hard as it was to watch his brother wallow in addiction over the years, he could only imagine the desperation he'd feel to fix a wife or a parent. "Is she sober now?"

"Yes. She finally got help a couple of years ago."

"Your dad never saw her whole."

A fresh wash of tears flooded her eyes, but she blinked hard and pushed them back. "No. And it cost him so much. Dmitri and I spent a lot of time at a support group when we were teenagers, and it was the only thing that kept us from being dragged under by the weight of Ma's problems. Dad never understood that he had to take care of himself until it was too late."

He glanced around her apartment, not really looking, but needing to free himself from her gaze, her intensity. "I can't let Danny fall, Andri. My parents have already given up, so without me, he's on his own."

"Have they given up? Or have they realized that they're collateral damage if they don't save themselves from his ruin and wreckage?"

That snapped his attention back to her. Was that what his dad had done? Pulled himself out of harm's way? For a moment, his thoughts whirled. What would that be like, to let go, to live each day without a rock of terrible speculation in his stomach, wondering what trouble his brother would find next? The allure of self-preservation beckoned to him, but his sense of honor and duty thickened around his battered heart.

She leaned forward, placed her cool hand over his where it rested on his thigh, and his heart jumped a little. He'd missed her touch. "Travis, you can offer support. Love him, unconditionally. But the rest has to be up to him. You can't do it for him. And it's painfully clear that you're trying to."

"My dad told me something very similar a few weeks ago." He sighed and drummed the fingers of his free hand against the arm of the sofa. He sat silent for a moment, relishing the sense of comfort he often felt in her company. He focused on the softness of her skin against his as she stroked his wrist with the pad of her thumb, all his nerve endings on high alert for more of her touch.

Then his thoughts tumbled past his lips before he could stop them. "I'm not sure I know how to stop fighting his addiction for him." For a sharp moment, he desperately wanted to stop, to just let go. But what kind of brother did that make him?

Andri pulled him back to her with a squeeze of her hand. "You've been doing this a long time?"

"Not long enough. I took good care of him for a while when he was young." After Jacob died, Travis had taken his responsibility seriously. He'd tried so hard to shield his little brother from everything painful and sad in life. But once he'd entered middle school, he'd avoided carrying the weight of Danny's happiness. It was too much, and he'd wanted freedom.

Though he'd hidden that part of himself all these years, he couldn't resist the urge to release this particular failing into her care. Somehow, he thought Andri would understand this, too. "When I got older, I stopped letting him hang out with me and my friends because he was my lame little brother and he'd get in the way of having fun. By the time I was seventeen or so, I realized that he needed me. I started trying to protect him. I think he was struggling with depression, even then. He tried to be bigger than life, always out doing crazy skateboard tricks, getting in trouble with his buddies, stuff like that. I thought he was acting out because he wanted attention from our mother, but maybe there was more to it."

"He's still battling depression?"

"Yes. He doesn't like the meds, though, so I think he self-medicates in his own way. It doesn't make sense to me, but, there it is." He turned his hand under hers, catching her fingers, threading their hands together. "Are we still friends?"

He half expected her to say no, but she smiled, cutting a path through the darkness shrouding him. "Of course."

God, he really loved that smile. "Then I think you should let me take you out tomorrow. Maybe give me a chance to prove to you that I really am a nice guy."

She laughed. "Travis, I know you're a nice guy."

The compliment flowed easily from her lips, but it warmed his heart anyway.

Chapter Eight

In her nearly month long job search, Andri scored five job interviews, three of which turned her down because she was overqualified. Two invited her back for a second interview, and one a third, but no job offer yet.

She saw Travis every day after she moved into her apartment. They met for lunch or dinner. They caught a couple of movies, hiked, explored the aviary and the zoo. Sometimes she tagged along while he ran errands. He wasn't a fly fisher, which she was willing to temporarily overlook, but they did get out on the water, spending an evening at the reservoir with a few of Rachel's friends. They attended one night of the Pioneer Day rodeo to cheer on a bull-riding cousin of his. Throughout it all, she found herself growing closer and closer to him, though she reminded herself constantly they were just friends, that they had fun together, nothing more.

She and Travis exchanged texts often. Usually goofy things, but she enjoyed them. On a Friday night near the end of the month, he sent a text.

Travis: *Pick you up at 7 tomorrow night? We'll be fashionably late.*

Tomorrow night? What did they have planned—

"Oh, no." She'd forgotten his mother's fundraiser event. She dashed off a quick message, lying through her teeth. *Sounds great, looking forward to it.*

She didn't bother to look in her closet. She'd attended a couple of formal events with Peter, but once they broke up, the dresses and the pathetic memories they held went to Goodwill. Not that having them now would have helped. The extra three inches on her hips meant they wouldn't have fit anymore. She sent an SOS to Rachel. *HELP. Holt fundraiser tomorrow, formal, nothing to wear.*

She paced for five minutes, waiting for a reply, nearly ready to call instead when the response came.

Rachel: *Relax, off work by 10, call u then 4 shopping.*

The next day, after four stops, Andri found herself in a boutique that held some promise. There was no time for alterations, so finding a dress that looked good and didn't drag on the ground unless she wore platform stilettos proved to be a challenge.

A blue gown Rachel found had promise, but lost out the moment the saleswoman presented a pale green silk one. The one-shoulder Grecian style made Rachel laugh at the stereotype, but Andri loved it. After finding some gorgeous low-heeled strappy shoes and a new clutch at yet another store, Rachel followed her home to help her get ready. She'd rarely seen Rachel made up, but the woman was talented with a makeup brush, leaving her with smoky eyes, just a hint of color across her cheekbones, and a really fabulous bronzed lipcolor. Andri drew her thick hair into a loose twist. Magic, Rachel assured her before she left. Not that it mattered, when her date was just a friend.

Yet, when Travis arrived, Andri had to stop before she opened the door and put a hand on the jamb to steady herself. Suddenly, it really did matter what he might think of her appearance. It flew in the face of wanting to stay just friends, but she desperately wanted him to look at her with heat in his gaze. She could use the confidence boost.

Once she got a grip, she pulled the door open. Travis wore a beautifully cut black tuxedo, with a silver-gray vest and long tie. Electric heat sparked into goosebumps across her skin. His sunglasses disappointed her. She needed to see his eyes, to read her reflection in them and know if Rachel had successfully helped her find her inner Cinderella.

As if reading her mind, Travis slid the sunglasses down. His gaze dropped to the floor-length hem of her gown and slowly glided up her body, till his eyes met her own. The answering fire in his sharp blue gaze stole the air from her lungs.

"My God, you look incredible." His voice was low and husky.

Her heart banged against her ribcage in response. "Thank you. I was about to say the same about you." She stepped onto the landing, pulling the door closed behind her. Travis stepped toward her, one corner of his mouth quirked into a smile.

Desperate to ease the thick tension filling her, Andri reached up and pretended to straighten his perfect tie. "Seems to me you said 'black' tie."

He grinned, capturing her fingers with his own. "Taking a walk on the wild side." He tucked her fingers into the crook of his arm and escorted her to a sleek forest-green sedan.

"Nice car."

He opened her door. "Thanks, it isn't mine. I borrow it from my dad on special occasions. The truck isn't quite appropriate for a dress like that." He leaned down close to tuck her dress into the car, meeting her eyes with a smoldering look, setting her blood to sizzling as he backed away and shut the door.

Yes, she'd wanted to see that heat, that desire in his gaze, but seriously, if he didn't stop looking at her like that, she might burst into flames. Heaven help her if he touched her. She'd char to a crisp.

* * * *

Travis attended several big charity functions a year, at his mother's insistence. Sometimes as a representative of Holt Construction. Sometimes as the prized son of an influential family. Always regardless of whether or not he wanted to attend. He simply did his duty.

Of countless events, he didn't recall ever feeling this sense of anticipation before. Anticipation edging into hunger every time he looked at Andri during the drive up the canyon.

They conversed lightly, about movies and music, favorite restaurants, places they wanted to see, crazy things they wanted to try sometime in their lives. That was one of the many things he enjoyed about Andri, how easily they talked, how they never ran out of things to say to each other. Yet there were times they were perfectly content to be quiet in each other's company.

He turned his thoughts back to keeping his latest mantra running in his head. Keep it light, keep it fun, enjoy her company, don't dig too deep, don't get too close. He didn't want to fail her, to hurt her.

Her whiskey voice tantalized him as they talked, but as they laughed together, desire melted into that strange kind of delight he always felt in her company. Similar to the old-friend comfort he felt in Rachel's presence, but decidedly not just friends.

The fundraiser was in full swing by the time they arrived. The Silver Lode hotel donated space for the fundraiser every year. The beautiful gardens were cluttered with people, spilling out from the ballroom. He took Andri's hand, twining his fingers through hers as they descended a paved walk into the flow of business power players, politicians, sports figures, actors and other local movers and shakers.

Scanning the crowd, it appeared nearly everyone who was anyone in the region had come. Mother must be pleased, and not just because a huge turnout meant a successful fundraiser. He'd noticed over the years that event planning seemed to stoke her inner fire. She glowed a bit brighter, had more bounce in her step as she worked to make her vision happen. Travis liked that side of his mother.

Every few feet, someone spoke to him. Travis introduced Andri, not resisting the surge of jealousy-tinged satisfaction rushing through his veins when other men gave her appraising looks. She held herself with dignity, carried on intelligent conversations, charmed the socks off everyone he shared her company with. Travis couldn't remember the last time he had been so proud of the woman on his arm, or smiled so much at one of these events.

He placed a hand on the small of her back and guided her through the crowd toward the small stage where his father stood.

Someone appeared beside him. "I'm happy to see you made it, Travis."

His mother, wrapped in ivory chiffon, had come to him, and for a moment, he froze. The slight smile on her artfully made-up face caught him off guard as much as her presence alone. "You know I'd never miss one of your events, Mother."

Her gaze switched to Andri, and he said, "Mother, you remember Andromeda Miller."

The smile brightening his mother's face as she shook hands with Andri confused the hell out of him. It actually looked genuine. "Of course, Rachel's friend, from the July Fourth festivities. So nice to see you again, dear."

Andri exchanged a few pleasantries with his mother, then excused herself from their company to find the restroom. He watched her walk toward the open ballroom doors for a moment, the gentle sway of her hips mesmerizing him until his mother cleared her throat.

He forced himself to look at her. "I'm sorry, what did you say?"

His mother's brow lifted, but a slight smile still remained. "I said, she's a lovely young woman. But I see you've already noticed that."

Standing under Sophia Holt's gaze seemed to shrink his collar to an uncomfortable tightness. "Yes, I've noticed. She's a good friend, and pleasant company."

"You do look like you're having fun for a change. Good for you."

And then it was over. A congressman joined them, instantly shifting his mother's focus away from him. He'd received his allotted shower of attention from the woman who brought him into the world, and it was far more direct than what she typically offered him at one of these things. She never gave him her complete attention, usually speaking while looking through him, watching the crowd lest she miss someone important to her cause who might need to be greeted. She'd actually focused on him, though it was likely Andri who made the difference.

Yes, Travis knew Andri was something special. It didn't require his mother noticing her to tell him that. How strange that she had, though. He had no idea what to make of it, and it left him unsettled. After years of craving and actively seeking his mother's attention, Andri got it with no effort at all. It shamed him to admit that made him a little jealous, a reaction that shocked him almost as his mother had.

* * * *

Andri made her way carefully through the sea of black coats and colorful gowns worn by well-heeled guests as she returned to the festivities. She spotted Travis in a section of the garden, speaking with another couple and a petite blonde woman she recognized as Georgia Grant, the Silver Lode hotel manager and one of Rachel's friends.

Travis looked in her direction as she joined the group, and he broke into a wide grin. Her heart jumped, her skin tingled, and suddenly she felt as if the crowd had vaporized and it was just the two of them in that garden. In that moment, she realized any hope she had of not falling for him was gone. *Too late.*

Georgia excused herself to check in with Travis's mother and Andri, snapping back to reality, waited for an introduction to the elegant couple standing beside Travis. He presented her to Curran and Victoria Shaw. "Mr. Shaw owns DCS GlobalTech. He's moving the company to Salt Lake and we're remodeling the office building."

She perked up, recognizing the company name, while the impeccably tuxedoed man grinned and shook her hand. "Please, both of you, call me Curran. We're old friends by now, aren't we, Travis?"

Travis laughed and looked down at Andri. "I suppose we are. We built his home and his sister's a few years back. That was one of the last jobs Rachel's dad, Sam, did before he retired."

"Sam's a good man," Curran said. "I'm glad to hear he's enjoying retirement. I keep telling Ian he should get his dad on the slopes with us sometime."

Andri's eyes widened and she giggled. "Oh, you are a brave man if you ski with Ian. He's insane on the snow."

"He is that, but Curran's a bit of a madman himself," Victoria said. "I refuse to go on some of his runs."

Andri returned Victoria's smile, then granted herself a good five seconds to envy the woman's tall frame, draped in a glamorous, strapless copper gown. She tuned back in on the conversation. Curran had a bit of an accent, though she couldn't quite place it.

"Do you know anything about the Naturalist Basin, Travis?" Curran asked. "I've heard it's fantastic, but I don't know if my nephew could handle the hike."

Travis frowned, thoughtful. "It's gorgeous, but it's over seven miles in from the trailhead. If you really want to take him, you might want to go on horses. There are a lot of restrictions to protect the area, though. No fires, primitive camping. I'd check with the forest service before you try it, just to be sure."

Victoria leaned into her husband's side. "Are you going to invite the womenfolk?"

Andri felt another touch of envy when Curran looked at his wife with absolute devotion. She'd give a good decade off her life to have a man look at her like that. "If you'd like," he said. "Or, you and Kelli can go indulge in a spa weekend before her wedding plans drive her completely mad."

Victoria laughed and turned to Andri. "His sister, Kelli, is getting married in October, and she's *this* close to tossing her plans out and eloping to Vegas."

Andri remembered all too well the frustration of planning a wedding. "Poor thing."

Victoria nodded. "I love your name, Andri. What do you do?"

"Thank you. I'm an unemployed computer geek. Network engineering, IT, support, that sort of thing."

Victoria's amber eyes lit up and she nudged her husband out of his conversation with Travis. "Sweetie." She pointed at Andri. "Network engineer."

Curran focused on her, morphing in a split second from devoted husband to business mogul. His aura of complete control got her immediate attention. "Experience?"

Andri pulled herself together in a microsecond, faced with what she instinctively recognized was an opportunity that might lead to a job. "Seven years, including four managing IT.

I specialize in cybersecurity, I can write a mean database, and I don't have an aversion to talking to people, even the ones with problems who want to yell at me."

The expression in Curran's green eyes intensified, and he chuckled. "I certainly prefer a tech guru with people skills. We need a good engineer but we also need an IT manager. Ours doesn't want to move with the company." He slipped a wallet from the pocket inside his jacket and withdrew a card. "Do you have a pen?"

She retrieved one from her clutch and accepted his card. He gave her a number to write down on the back, and then said, "That's Jamie Mickleson's number. He's the CEO. Call him Monday morning, tell him I sent you."

She couldn't help the smile threatening to split her face. "Thank you, I will."

The evening passed in a blur. Andri tried the wonderful appetizers from the trays held by roving wait-staff, and Travis introduced her to so many people she doubted she'd remember any of the names other than the Shaws.

Watching Travis navigate with ease through the powerful crowd, the difference in their upbringing became even more apparent. He knew a ridiculous number of the guests, and made connections with new people rapidly. He picked up on conversation topics quickly, because he seemed to remember something of value about each person and their work or their families or their passions. She admired such adept people skills.

Andri had been a shy child, and Dmitri had warned her that she'd better learn to act happy and outgoing, or she wouldn't make any friends. Between that advice, and training herself to let his teasing roll off her back, she was able to survive just about any social situation, but she shuddered to think how out of place she'd feel tonight without that sort of life training.

She and Travis ate dinner in the ballroom, sampling foods from the nearest of a dozen or more buffet tables, and the chatting with other guests continued through the meal as the crowd shifted and flowed. Andri let Travis guide her through the evening's festivities. After spending some time in the main garden area, listening to a very funny comedian perform, Travis wrapped an arm around her waist and escorted her back into the ballroom. The tables had been cleared and chairs rearranged just in time for the auction, the highlight of Sophia Holt's event.

As they took their seats, Andri turned to Travis. "Wait, it's an actual auction? I thought these things were usually the silent sort."

Travis grinned and gently brushed a stray lock of hair off her forehead with his fingertips. Such a small thing, a light touch, yet it seared her skin and made it hard to concentrate as he spoke. "That would be more civilized, but Mother decided that having an open auction where people egged each other on to higher bids would be better for the overall fundraising effort. It's definitely more fun this way."

Sure enough, bidding at the auction grew spirited, not just in the interest of the children's hospital the proceeds were destined for, but for the sheer competition. Travis bid on several items, building the prices higher and higher, but bowing out before he actually purchased anything. Andri watched him, enjoying the lively spark of competition in his eyes. She had no idea if he could possibly afford to pay the price if he pushed too far and won, but the longer she watched, the more she saw his shrewdness. He never pushed his luck and he knew exactly when to back down. She hadn't seen this side of him before, and it fascinated her.

The bidding for a unique bronze piece, sculpted for the auction by one of Utah's most renowned artists, grew heated, and Travis was in the middle, stirring it along. Curran Shaw called across the aisle, "Mate, I don't think you really want that piece, you're just driving up the price. You've been doing it all night."

Travis faced Curran, his lips turned up in a sly grin. "Possibly. I might be trying to soak you for all you're worth in the name of a good cause. If you think that's so, why don't you stop bidding and concede the piece to me?"

Victoria Shaw laughed and shook her head, dark curls bouncing. Curran studied Travis for a moment, until the auctioneer said, "Going once."

"What the hell, it is a good cause." Curran broke into a smile, then waved at the auctioneer. "Thirty-five thousand."

Travis nodded at his nemesis. "It's all yours, sir."

The audience laughed, and the auctioneer quickly wrapped up the bid. "Sold!"

After the auction, people began leaving. The sky darkened, chasing away the last of the paint the setting sun had tossed on the sky above the western mountains as Travis guided Andri through the crowd.

A slim, sandy-haired man sporting a goatee and a double-breasted gray tuxedo approached from a side path. "Travis Holt, you've proven difficult to reach lately." The man's smile brought to mind a late-night infomercial host: blindingly white, smarmy and altogether fake.

Andri saw Travis's irritation in the way his jaw clenched. "Mr. Jasper. What can I do for you?"

Ah, that was it. Travis had regaled her with tales of the finicky Craig Jasper. He'd been thrilled last week to finally close on the man's house. The one she'd worked on the day she literally fell into Travis's arms.

Travis had refused to talk business on behalf of the family company throughout the evening, at least when she'd been beside him. While she appreciated his devotion of time to her, Andri decided it might be best for Travis to talk to Mr. Jasper now so he didn't have to later in the week, when something really important might have to be infringed upon.

She slid her fingers out of his hand. "Travis, if you'll excuse me for a moment, I'm going to grab a drink before everything is cleaned up."

He nodded, his gaze unreadable. "I'll find you when I'm finished."

She left him enduring his client. At one of the tables along the garden path, she picked up a diet cola and a tiny chocolate confection she knew would add to her hips before she even tasted it. She popped the sinful dessert in her mouth. Calories be damned. Life was too short not to eat chocolate.

Life was too short not to enjoy a lot of things that weren't particularly good for her. Like Travis. She couldn't help it. They fit together in such interesting ways, with so many similar interests. He'd quickly become one of the best friends she'd ever had, but lately it was getting harder and harder to keep the physical attraction under control. The more she knew him, understood him, enjoyed him, the more she found herself craving him. How was she going to work around that?

She sipped her drink as she wandered up the walkway, exchanging goodbyes with a few people she'd met. By the time she finished her drink and disposed of the cup, Andri found herself at an amazing fountain. Strands of tiny white lights strung in the nearby trees twinkled like a fairy garden and reflected in the water tumbling over the spiral structure.

Staring at the water, she revisited the idea of being more than just friends with Travis. It came to mind every now and again, especially since his slightest touch sent her hormones bouncing around. But she repeatedly pushed it back. Number one, her life was still too unstable to be messing around with a relationship. She needed a job, needed to be standing fully on her own two feet before she got involved with anyone.

Worse, number two, he didn't want more than friendship. She knew she got to him. The flashes of heat and desire in his eyes told her so, as did the possessive way he sometimes pulled him to her, only to let it turn into a friendly hug because he didn't want anything more. And she hadn't forgotten a single detail of his kiss after their first date. But he had his own reasons for staying just friends. He bore the weight of huge responsibilities right now, and she knew he'd been hurt before.

Number three, Danny. He was a great big roadblock all on his own.

Enough already. There was no sense in twisting herself into knots when going with the flow was the only option she really had. They were friends, definitely. At the moment, Andri couldn't reconcile where benefits would fit into their lives without creating additional problems neither of them needed. That idea went back on the furthest, coolest burner on her mental stove. She released all her thoughts to the warm evening breeze, losing herself in the rushing fountain's music.

* * * *

Night spread through the sky above Travis. In the light of old fashioned lamps on posts throughout the hotel's gardens, small groups of people still gathered, talking, laughing. Travis quickened his pace, his need to feel Andri beside him increasing as the minutes passed. He ignored the warning in his head. Being with her, talking with her, touching her filled him up, brightening his dark soul, and his internal mantra of *keep it light, don't get too close* grew quieter.

He got a lucky break. One of the couples he'd introduced Andri to earlier in the evening had seen her recently, and pointed him in the right direction. He passed through a vine-covered arch and spotted her standing by a fountain. He crossed the walkway quietly, trying not to disturb whatever her thoughts might be. He stopped a few feet from her, letting the vision of her fill his senses.

She faced away from him, staring at the tumbling water. Her gown swirled around her in the evening breeze, outlining her legs, the curve of her hips. The bare skin of her shoulder and upper back made his fingers ache to touch her, to caress the silkiness of her shoulder, the curve of her neck, to catch her vanilla scent as he kissed her nape. The tiny lights dancing on the trees glinted off her dark hair, the thick, loose twist calling to him. Her hair should be loose, free, in his hands.

He got less than a foot from her before she realized someone was there and stiffened. Before she could turn around, he shushed her. "It's just me, Andri."

She relaxed and turned her head slightly, watching him in her peripheral vision. He grasped one of the few stray tendrils of hair floating across her back, twining it around his finger, the strands silky smooth, then released it. He set his hands on her shoulders, and she shivered. Her soft skin tempted him. Travis trailed his thumbs gently down her spine to her waist, then ran his fingertips up again. The silken texture of her skin matched that of her dress, a sensation nearly too much for his control. His breathing quickened, his heart pounding like he'd run here to the fountain. He tightened his grip on her shoulders, winding in his desire a bit.

"You owe me one for leaving me by myself with the most annoying client of the decade." He tried to mask the edge of want in his voice, and knew he failed.

She trembled when he shifted nearer, so close behind her yet not quite touching. "It seemed best to let you talk business alone," she said, her grainy voice wavering.

Travis laughed softly. "I think I've talked enough." He ran a hand along her throat, up under her chin, tilting her head to the side to give him access. He couldn't resist tasting her there, to see if she was still as sweet as he remembered.

The sound of her gasp sent a tremor down his spine as he pressed his lips to the heated, tender skin along the side of her neck. The vanilla fragrance, so completely hers, wrapped around him as he slid his other hand down her arm and across her waist, pulling her tight against him, his chest pressed to her back.

He trailed kisses along her neck and jaw, his pulse roaring in his ears, his groin stirring. Her soft, small hand spread against the back of his hand, pressing his palm hard to her abdomen. Every muscle in his body cranked tighter and he rested his chin on her shoulder, fighting inside to master his desire before he lost it completely.

He released her chin and raised his hand to her mass of hair. His fingers found a pin and eased it from the thick strands. As he released the second one, she shivered in his arms. His awareness of her grew acute and he refused to think, to reason beyond this perfect moment.

He nuzzled her ear, the scent of her sweet and exotic and entirely intoxicating. "I want my hands in your hair," he murmured, then flicked his tongue along her earlobe. She said nothing, her breath catching, but her hand met his, pulling pins loose. He took the pins from her, dropping them in his pocket. She sifted through her hair with her fingers, and the heavy dark waves tumbled down across his shoulder and neck, touching a chord deep inside him, drawing a groan past his lips. Heated memories of his dreams, of her wrapped around him, surfaced hard and strong.

Travis pulled her around to face him, the need to taste her more than he could bear. Her eyes, huge and deep, searched his and she curled a hand around the back of his neck. Her touch yanked his control over the breaking point. With his arm around her waist and his other hand knotting into her mass of hair, Travis lowered his mouth over hers.

Their lips touched, held, then melded. Electricity ripped through his body when she responded to him. He felt her slip a hand inside his jacket and up his back, and Andri wrapped her other arm around his neck, pulling him securely to her. The pressure of every sweet curve filled him, overwhelmed him. He drew the tip of his tongue across the seam of her lips.

A whimper escaped her. She parted her lips beneath his, and he deepened the kiss. The faint taste of cola and chocolate on her tongue overloaded his already buzzing senses, and he lost awareness of anything beyond her mouth, her body. He felt her weaken in his arms, her fingers flexing and tightening on his shirt, his neck. He slid his hand down from her waist, pulling her hips flush against him. Her breath hitched, and in that moment he knew he was lost.

Panic clamped around his heart. He broke the kiss and lifted his head, suddenly unable to breathe. God, what had he done? He'd allowed himself to blur the borders of their friendship and the price for both of them loomed in his head. He gently, deliberately disentangled himself from her arms.

She looked up at him, dark eyes still hazy with desire, a smile on her soft lips. Her expression told him she had no idea she'd stripped his heart bare, no idea she held the power to crush him. God help him, he didn't want her to know. He'd known he was flirting with danger, but spending time with her felt so damned good. She was everything he needed, everything he wanted. But the potential they had to hurt each other sent the scale so far out of balance, how could he possibly justify anything other than friendship?

The breeze kicked up stronger then, cooler, sending a shiver through her, giving him the way out he desperately needed. "It's getting chilly. I'd better get you to the car."

"You do a fine job of keeping me warm," she said, her low, whiskey voice luring his body.

Panic shifted into higher gear. He took a deep breath, searching inside for something to barricade himself. Anger at himself for allowing things to go a little too far rose, but he refused to wield that against her. Instead, he reached for a grin.

"Andri, it's time to take you home. Chivalry isn't dead, you know. I'm supposed to protect you from things that lurk in the night."

Her dark eyes flashed and she smiled again. "Things like you?"

Oh, if she only knew. He shook his head and took her hand. "Come on."

Chapter Nine

Travis regretted kissing her. Andri watched him during the drive home from the fundraiser, and the regret flickered in his eyes and threaded through his voice, even as he laughed and talked with her. She kept the conversation light for his sake, though his obvious remorse tore at her.

No one had kissed her like Travis did. Ever. Not even close. His heat still imprinted her, searing her all the way to her toes. She struggled to keep her mind on the conversation, not on the memory of his strong hands or the sure way he had taken possession of her. He could have taken her right there in that secluded spot in the garden, if he wanted to. Could have her now, if he asked.

He'd never ask.

She replayed the scene over in her head, reliving the sensations of Travis holding her, the need she felt in his kiss. She lingered on the heat of his mouth, the hardness of his muscles under her fingers, the possessive way he pulled her to him.

It left her aching, body and soul. But something had yanked him out of the moment, and she wished she understood what. The ugly little thoughts that fed her inadequacies filtered into her head.

She'd told Rachel she didn't have any man skills. She never kept a man's interest beyond a few of months. Men seemed to like her, or at least like part of her, until they got to know her better. Some drifted away, with calls or texts or online messages dying off gradually. Others were more direct, and she'd heard 'it's not you, it's me' enough to figure it probably *was* her. Seeing them move on to someone else who really did make them happy solidified it. Her man skills sucked. She shoved the mental snakes to the back of her mind, refusing to feed them as they coiled and hissed.

Parked in front of her apartment building, Travis switched off the ignition, leaving them in the dark, his face outlined by the sidewalk light. He stared out his window, tension filling the air between them. "Travis," she said softly. "Look at me."

His gaze met hers as she ran her fingers over his where they clenched the steering wheel. "It was just a kiss, Travis. It was a great kiss, but that's all. Don't regret it, because that just makes me feel inadequate."

She couldn't breathe, watching distress and a hint of anger cloud his eyes. His gaze went to her mouth and held. He reached over and drew his fingers along her cheek, pulling the ache inside her to a peak. *Oh, please kiss me.*

Travis ran his thumb across her lower lip, then dropped his hand from her face and got out of the car. He gave her a smile that didn't gleam in his eyes when he helped her out, tucking her hand into the crook of his arm as he walked her up to her apartment.

Andri's thoughts churned. She wasn't sure what to do, but instinct told her if he left with this uncertainty hanging between them, something vital in their relationship would be irretrievably lost. She unlocked her door and turned back to him.

Travis said, "I had a great time, Andri. The best ever at one of my mother's events."

His broad shoulders were stiff with tension, his dark blue gaze conflicted. Her heart pounded, pulsing in her ears, as he stared at her mouth for a moment, then shifted back on his heel, ready to turn away. Watching him leave suddenly became unbearable. "Travis?"

He froze. "What?"

What did she think she could say? Please don't leave? I want you? She'd hit something inside him, something he pulled back to protect. How did she work past that?

She drew a shaky breath, then stepped forward and smoothed the lapel of his jacket. "Come in for a while."

He watched her, his expression clouded, the muscle in his jaw clenching. A man at war with his thoughts. Finally, he stepped forward, pushed the door open, and waved her in.

Travis followed her, sinking onto the sofa with her. He sat stiffly, hands on his thighs, and she wondered how to proceed. She was making this up as she went along, and now she wondered what she was doing. As much as she feared sacrificing herself in a relationship that would be a ménage between her, him, and his pain, she wasn't ready to let the possibility of being with Travis vanish.

She took his hand in hers, feeling the calluses on his palms under her fingertips. He ran his thumb over her knuckles and a slow burn ignited deep inside her belly, swirling in time with the motion of his thumb. She licked her lips, a thrill shivering across her skin when his gaze focused on her mouth. Then he shook his head once. He lifted her hand, pressed his lips to her knuckles, and released her. "I'd better go."

No, that's not what she wanted. Her brain flew through options in the seconds between when he spoke and she responded, "Why?"

He laughed softly. "Why? Honestly? Because if I stay, I don't think we'll be friends for long."

Her stomach flipped. He felt the heat, too. Good. For once in her life, she was going to dig into the source code of a relationship and program it to do what she wanted it to. "I have an idea."

His brows lifted. "What sort of an idea?"

She sat up, leaning toward him slightly. "Neither one of us is looking for a serious relationship right now."

"True."

"But I'll be honest with you, Travis. I've been really lonely for a long time now, even before I found out my engagement was a farce. Feeling alone when you're with someone hurts even more than just being alone, you know?" She laid her hand on Travis's thigh and watched the hunger she'd been hoping for fill his gaze. "I'd bet my life savings that you're every bit as lonely."

He swallowed hard. "I am. But I see where you're headed with this, and it's not a good idea."

"Oh, you think not? Tell me something. Do you think about kissing me in your truck?"

His expression grew pained. "Constantly."

"So do I. Look, we're both intelligent adults here. We like each other, we get along, we clearly have chemistry. We don't have to fall into anything if we choose not to. We can take care of each other, enjoy each other's company. Like, friends with benefits."

He shook his head, his tension visible. "It won't work. Do you know how many movies have been made with that premise? We won't stay friends. The whole thing will implode."

"No, it won't. We'll be careful. We won't abuse the privilege of benefits." She traced her fingers up his arm, along his shoulder, down to his chest. She reveled in the hard heat of the muscles beneath his snowy shirt. "Travis, I haven't been touched in four years. I need your hands on me."

He ran his fingertips down the side of her face, then slid his hand into the mass of hair at her nape, his stormy gaze locking onto hers. The intense desire radiating from him was unmistakable and cranked her own to a fever pitch. *Please say yes, please, please.*

Travis wrapped her hair around his hand and her breath caught. He shifted closer, tilted her chin up with his other hand, the warmth of his skin feeding the flame inside her. He brushed his lips over hers, once, twice, then held, sinfully gentle. The rushing sound of her pulse grew stronger in her ears, as he caressed her lips with his own.

"Promise me you won't hate me in the morning." His words vibrated against her mouth.

Could she ever hate him? "I promise."

His mouth captured hers again, harder, his tongue seeking entry. She moaned, deep in her throat, as her lips parted, welcoming him.

He tasted her, exploring her mouth in a slow seduction that made her ache for more. Travis held her to him, kissing along her jaw, down her throat as she dropped her head back. The heat of his mouth sent Andri's pulse soaring, and she reveled in the iron grip of his arm around her, curling her fingers around the hard bicep beneath his tuxedo jacket. Goosebumps shivered onto her skin in the wake of his hand caressing her back, her waist, her bottom. She pressed her palm to his jaw, bringing his lips back to hers.

The rasp of his tongue against hers, the nip of his teeth on her lower lip sent waves of delicious tension rippling through her, coursing over and under her skin. He drew his fingers up, tracing her rib cage, finally closing over her breast, and her flesh tightened in response, every nerve ending alive and tingling. She gasped, arching into his touch. Oh, she'd needed this, needed *him*, so much! He swirled his thumb over her taut nipple through the layers of silk separating his skin from hers, sending white hot bolts of desire straight through her belly, leaving her throbbing.

Breathing hard, he pulled back, his eyes hot. "Come on." He rose from the sofa, pulling her up by the hand. He kissed her, then grabbed her, swinging her up into his arms. "I've dreamed of doing this since I caught you when you fell."

She loosened the knot on his tie, sliding it from his neck as he carried her down the hall and pushed open her bedroom door with his foot. He set her on her feet at the side of the bed, shrugging out of his tuxedo jacket and letting it drop to the floor as she worked the buttons of his shirt and vest. Soon, those fell to the floor as well, and she ran her hands over the smooth skin and hard muscles. She'd enjoyed her own little lust-fest over his chest since the day she'd watched him coat his firm pecs and golden skin with sunscreen. Touching him beat the hell out of any fantasy.

His hands settled at her waist, fingers stroking along her sides until his left hand found the zipper of her dress. He tugged, growling with obvious frustration when the zipper refused to move. She smiled and threaded her fingers into his hair, pulling him down to kiss him while she gripped the top of the dress with her other hand, allowing the zipper to move when he tugged again. "There," she said. "Teamwork."

"I like teamwork." He ran his fingers under the edge of the strap on her gown, pulling it over her shoulder. He drew it slowly down her arm and she shuddered as the fabric slithered over her hips, puddling at the floor when he released it, leaving her bare except for silky pink panties and the shoes she started to slip off.

He stopped her with a hand on her waist. "Keep the shoes."

The erotic suggestion melted her, leaving her wet and wanting.

"Andromeda." The rough edge in his voice, the near reverence in his tone, sent a delicious shiver down her spine, matching the electricity generated as his calloused hands skimmed over her bare breasts. "You are beautiful."

Andri smiled, as warm inside from his sweet words as she was outside from his touch. She backed up a half-step, then lay back on the bed, shifting her hair out from under her back. Eyes darkening as he watched her, Travis stripped off his pants and stretched out beside her.

She touched the beautifully carved muscles of his chest, thrilled at the combination of heat and hardness, suddenly craving the feel of him in her hand. Andri slid her hand down his torso, but he grabbed her hand before she reached her destination.

Travis shook his head. "In a minute." He lifted her arms up over her head, locking the fingers of one hand around her wrists. "Let me touch you," he murmured, sending off another ripple of desire to pulse between her thighs.

"Please do," she whispered, her voice catching on a gasp as he nuzzled her, kissing her neck, her breast. His tongue flicked and swirled against her flesh, a moan escaping her. He trailed his fingertips from her collarbone down over her breast, her stomach, her lower abdomen. He released his grip on her wrists as he shifted down and she explored the muscles along his arm, his shoulder.

She sucked in a shuddering breath and flexed her hips as he ventured lower, encouraging him to please, please get there, almost, *oh, God, yes.* He took his maddeningly sweet time, his touch gentle as he explored, discovered, tasted, until she was trembling with need. And then everything inside her surged, peaked, exploded in climax.

Travis slid up her body, skin against skin, chest against breast, his smile full of primal pride, his gaze brimming with desire. Suddenly, his expression dimmed. "Damn. Andri, I wasn't expecting this. I'm not a good Boy Scout."

It took a moment for her brain to register his words and translate. No protection. He wasn't carrying condoms. The intense satisfaction that bloomed in her heart at the thought that he'd been celibate so long he didn't bother with an emergency packet in his wallet surprised her. "That's okay. I was a very successful Girl Scout." Bad periods had meant years of the pill. "We're good to go."

He grinned. "Glad to hear it, because I really, really don't want to stop."

She grabbed his neck, pulling him down to her, kissing him hard. "Please, don't stop. Don't you dare."

He braced his weight on one forearm, slid his hand along her thigh, and slowly entered her, giving her time to adjust. The fullness, the sense of completion, took her breath away. She wrapped her arms around him, rocking her hips against him, and he took her cue. She welcomed him, relishing the way he fit her. As the rhythm built, she recognized and accepted how very, truly, deeply lost she was.

The realization colored her building excitement with the understanding that, whether he returned her feelings or not, a relationship with this man would likely be painful. She chose to take the chance, to risk misery in exchange for being with the man she saw struggling to shoulder the weight of his life. She'd simply have to take every moment as it happened and work to keep some sort of wall up between his suffering and her need to carry it for him.

She teetered on the edge of bliss, distracted by her thoughts until he surged against her, groaning her name. The thrill engulfed her and she came with him.

* * * *

Sunday morning, Travis woke to the sound of movement in his room. He cracked an eye open and caught sight of Andri, all tousled hair and lovely skin and a truly outstanding ass. Oh, yeah, not his room. Hers. She slipped into the adjoining bathroom, closing the door with a tiny click. He stared at the blank white ceiling for a moment, trying to engage his brain rather than think with his growing erection.

The kiss by the fountain had done it. He knew for certain then they were more than friends. No. If he was honest with himself, he'd known there was more for a long time. After that kiss, he couldn't deny his own truth any longer. For all her 'friends with benefits' talk last night, he was willing to bet she knew they were much more than friends, too. He growled at himself and tossed back the tangled sheets, making his way into the hall and the second bathroom.

The situation churned through his mind as he cleaned up. He wanted her around. Pure and simple. He'd let her down, of course. Somehow. He always did. He'd lost Jacob, destroying his mother's love for him and ripping it away from Danny in the process. He'd failed in his marriage, made the colossal mistake of tying himself to Melody, and had his heart crushed under her favorite designer heels the day she moved out. Travis needed to push Andri away, but he searched inside himself and failed to find the part that could do it.

The truth was, no matter how brutally they would likely both hurt each other down the road, he needed her. And, God help him, he wanted her, too. So, headlong into the abyss he went.

When Travis returned to Andri's room, he found her sitting on the end of the bed. Her hands rested in her lap, fingers curled into the hem of the enormous t-shirt she'd put on. Tension radiated from her, and for a moment, he worried that she regretted asking him to make love to her. He resisted that thought, realizing when her chin came up and her gaze sought his that it was fear of him turning on her that churned in her head.

His heart twisted hard as he recognized her fear. He had to reassure her. The time would come when he hurt her, but it wasn't going to be now, and it damn well wasn't going to be on purpose. He could fix this.

He sat beside her, picked up one of her hands, wrapped it in his own. "You know, your mom's going to be seriously pissed at me. She did want you to attend Sunday services, and here I am, keeping you otherwise occupied."

Andri laughed softly. "Oh, Ma would rant and rave if she knew you'd slept over. Missing church would be a far distant second."

Travis pulled her into his side with an arm around her shoulders, giving her a gentle squeeze and pressing a kiss into her shower-damp hair. He ran a hand up her thigh, toying with the hem of her t-shirt. He slid her hair aside and kissed the gentle slope between neck and shoulder, tasting her skin, breathing in the intriguing scent of vanilla and Andri. When she exhaled and the tension melted from her body, he smiled. This would end one day, yes. Painfully, he had no doubt. But for now, they were fine, everything was okay. "Let's get dressed. I want to take you home with me."

She pulled back to look at him. "What's the plan?"

"Not sure I know yet. But you might want to follow me in your car. I'd hate to head for work in the morning and leave you stranded."

"Sounds good." She grinned, warming his heart in a flash before she hurried to dress.

* * * *

After a quick stop to trade his dad's car for the truck—during which dad greeted Andri warmly, grinning from ear to ear—Travis took Andri home. His chalet sat on a hill overlooking the picturesque town of Midway, nestled into the foothills of the Wasatch Back. The log-walled house had few rooms, but each of them went a bit overboard on square footage. He couldn't help it, he needed space to breathe.

He shifted his tuxedo jacket to his left hand and unlocked the door, wondering if Andri noticed his hands trembling. Ah, no, she was checking out the skyline, the surrounding mountains scraping the brilliant blue sky. He forced a bit more control over himself to steady his hands. Amazing that bringing a woman home for the first time would make him nervous, but it was suddenly a matter of great importance that she like his personal space.

He pushed open the door and reached for her hand. "Welcome, Ms. Miller. The grand tour begins momentarily."

"I can hardly wait." She grinned at him, and his stomach flipped in a way that left him a bit dazed. He could look at that smile every day for the rest of his life and never grow tired of it.

She followed him into the house. He lifted a hand to indicate the room. "Here we have the main room. Living area and entertainment space in one." She glanced from the stark leather and wood furniture to the rough rock fireplace extending up the wall to the top of the vaulted ceiling. She nodded at the plasma television he rarely used, then stepped over to the far wall of the open space and trailed her finger along one of the built in bookcases. "Oh, very nice, Mr. Holt. You have a decent library, and...oh, this is cool." She stopped at the shelves crammed with vinyl records. She crouched to slide album covers out and explored his collection a moment before turning a bright smile his way. "You have some seriously awesome stuff here."

Giddy. Yeah, that was a word that fit the silly happiness bouncing through him. A girl liked his vinyl collection. Surely he hadn't generated enough good karma in his life to deserve this. "Thanks. I've had a lot of them since I was a teenager, gifts from my Uncle Mac's collection. I try to stop at yard sales and I troll the internet for new ones sometimes." She pulled out a couple of glam rock LPs from the early 80s. "I found those at Deseret Industries a couple of years ago."

Andri laughed. "Never know what treasures you'll find at the D.I. It was always my favorite place to go thrifting in college."

"Come on, the tour continues." He held out a hand and she accepted it, allowing him to pull her up. She heartily approved of the kitchen and his supply of restaurant-quality pots and pans on the suspended cast iron rack. The main bath, guest bedroom, and office space completed the main floor. She admired his choice of wireless network router more than his kitchen setup. "You must get full signal halfway down the street. Please tell me it's secure."

"Yes, ma'am. With a nice, long, complicated password." He laughed when she patted him on the head and nodded approval.

His heart skipped a beat as he ushered her to the curving staircase, leading up to the loft. "The master bedroom takes up the loft."

Her gaze slid into his, all warmth and light. "Does the tour include the loft, then, or are you just mentioning it in passing?"

He touched her waist, ran his palm to the small of her back. "That depends. If I take you up there, will you help me break in the bed?"

Andri's elegant brows lifted as she drew her fingers down along the buttons of the same white shirt she'd helped him out of last night. He'd have never believed it if someone had told him to make sure he had a change of clothes, just in case. "Is the bed new? Or are you trying to tell me that it's new to being used by two people?"

He curled his fingers around hers, lifted them to his mouth, caught one between his teeth. She gasped, desire shimmering in her eyes. "I built this place after my divorce. The only women who've set foot inside are my mother, twice, and

Rachel, but she doesn't really count, and she's never been upstairs, other than when she did the electrical work."

"Hmm." She tilted her head to the side, withdrew her fingers from his grasp and caressed his cheek and jaw, warming his heart as effectively as she ratcheted up his need for her. "You know, this is definitely a man's home. I mean, you don't even have curtains. Not that wood blinds are bad, but still. It tells me a lot about your need for a woman's touch."

"Oh, does it?" The sudden vision of his home mixing with the eclectic nods to decorating in her apartment filled him with delight. Damn, he was completely gone over this girl. He shoved away the nagging self-doubt that reared its ugly head. "You know, I do have one decorative item you might like. It's upstairs."

"With the bed."

"Yes."

"Then I suppose you had better lead on and let me see your more decorative side."

He inclined his head, waving his hand up the stairs. "After you, my dear."

She climbed the stairs and he knew the moment she laid eyes on his decorative side, as she put it. "Oh, Travis. Now that is spectacular."

He followed her to the right wall. Between the door to the closet and the door to the master bathroom, the wall housed a massive saltwater aquarium. A rainbow of brilliant fish swam among corals and anemones, giving his home color and a bit of life besides his own, lending his bedroom some measure of peace. "You like it?"

"It's gorgeous. The colors are amazing, purple and yellow and red...so vibrant. Oh, look at the black clown fish. I love those."

He set his hands on her shoulders, ran his fingers lightly down her back until she shivered and turned to him, giving him a quick hug before she stepped around him to explore the rest of the loft. Beyond the half wall, the loft was open to the main room below. It was lit at the moment by diffuse sunlight from the huge north-facing windows along the third wall.

She faced the king-size bed. "Very nice." A flare of heat raced across his skin when she sat on the bed, then stretched out across it. "It's bigger than mine."

He grinned and unbuttoned his shirt. "Mmm-hmm. I think we can put it to good use."

Andri laughed, her grainy voice sending electric threads swirling and sparking through him. He ached for her, but took his time pulling off his clothes, determined to wring every ounce of pleasure from every moment of making love to his woman, including all the foreplay she could endure.

He lay beside her, naked, intending to kiss every inch of her as he removed her clothing. His intentions flew out the window when she stripped off her t-shirt and shimmied out of her shorts in record time, then settled herself between his knees. "What are you doing, Andri?" His blood pressure skyrocketed when she gave him a deliciously wicked grin and wrapped her fingers around him.

"I'm giving you, and your poor, lonely bed, what you both need. A woman's touch." He groaned when she put her mouth to work on him, beginning a very long, completely consuming, utterly satisfying afternoon that succored every neglected thing—his bed, his body, and his heart.

* * * *

She braced herself. Andri regretted waking after nights when she dreamed of Travis, losing the remnants of him to the morning sun. Then she opened her eyes and pleasure burst inside her, glowing to the tips of her fingers and toes.

Two mornings in a row, it wasn't a dream.

She stretched in Travis's huge bed, then snuggled back into the pillow that smelled like him, listening to the sound of water running in the shower. She felt amazing, truly satisfied from head to toe. They had spent Sunday breaking in the bed. And the couch. And the kitchen countertop. Oh, and then there was the shower, that amazing marble shower with the built-in seat and the full-body shower heads. She knew every inch of his beautiful form now, and he knew hers.

One more thing she knew: she'd never be able to let him go. Not that she was ready to admit it to *him*. But tucking that truth away in her heart didn't make it any less true. It merely gave her what she, in her darkest thoughts, understood was a false sense of security: the idea that she wouldn't be hurt so bad when things fell apart if she didn't actually tell him how much she felt for him.

The water stopped and Travis emerged in a cloud of steam from the bathroom, rubbing a towel through his hair. He quietly opened a few drawers, pulling out clothing, seeming unaware of her state of consciousness. She watched him move as he dressed, admiring the muscles flexing across his back, along his shoulders and down through his legs as he stepped into his trousers. There was something undeniably sexy about watching Travis dress, but she quieted the stirring inside her. If he didn't absolutely have to go into the office, he'd still be laying beside her. She silently extracted a promise from herself not to delay him.

He reached into the closet for a pale blue shirt, then turned toward her while he fastened the buttons. His gaze met hers, and his lips curved into a genuinely happy smile. "Morning."

"Hey, handsome."

Travis tucked his shirt in, fastened his trousers, then sat down beside her. He leaned down, the clean smell of his skin enticing her, and kissed her on the forehead.

She growled at him. "I'm trying very hard not to climb all over you, you know."

He grinned. "Believe me, getting out of that bed has never been more difficult." He got up and walked over to the dresser. He searched under folded socks for a while, found what he wanted and said, "Here."

He tossed something onto her blanket-covered stomach. Andri picked up the key, excitement coiling in her stomach. "Is this an invitation?"

Travis's eyes narrowed, his grin turned slightly wicked. "No, sweetheart, it's a demand. I expect you to be here when I get home tonight. Just lock up when you leave to do whatever you're going to do to while away the hours."

"You're taking an awful lot for granted, Mr. Holt." She yawned and stretched, relishing the blatant desire on his face when the covers fell away from her. "What are your plans for tonight?"

His gaze turned positively predatory and his voice dropped a notch. "Oh, just let your imagination run wild. I'm sure you'll cover it."

The thrill rolling inside took her breath away. He shook his head and said, "I'm not going to kiss you goodbye, because if I do, I'll never get out that door, and I have a meeting in an hour. See you later, Andri."

She waved, watched him descend the stairs, listened to the door open and close. Andri threw herself back on the bed, staring at the ceiling. Life was good. No, definitely an understatement. Everything felt perfect.

* * * *

Travis drove, his mind divided between navigation and the woman he'd left in his bed. He thought he'd forgotten how to feel, but Andri pulled something vital from the dark recesses of his soul. He needed her, needed the freedom he felt with her. She made it possible for him to breathe again, and he wanted her on a level so deep he didn't even try to question it. It had been a very long time since he felt so strongly about anyone, not since Melody—

Light flooded through him, a chill shivering down his spine. Correction. Melody never did this to him. The way Andri affected him was like that rusty proverb about lightning only striking once. What were the chances he'd ever feel like this again? He'd be an utter fool to let her slip away.

Travis pulled into the parking lot at the Holt Construction offices, somehow refreshed and far more ready to face the day than when he'd climbed into the truck.

Chapter Ten

By the following Saturday, Andri was tired to the bone, and if she hadn't promised Rachel a girls night, she'd collapse and sleep for twelve hours. She'd worked at GlobalTech for all of five days, but they were viciously long days. The company was under a very tight schedule to coordinate the switch from Los Angeles to Salt Lake City, turning L.A. into a satellite office while company headquarters moved.

She'd aced her interview and been hired on Monday, only to find herself dropped in the deep end of the pool on Tuesday morning when she realized just how much work lay ahead. Granted, she put most of the pressure on herself, but she wanted the systems done right, rush to finish notwithstanding. Garbage in meant garbage out, so if she didn't want greater headaches later, she'd make sure everything was as perfect as possible from the ground up, hardware and software.

As a result, her job took over her life. She worked nearly every waking hour and she hadn't seen Travis since Tuesday morning. She missed him with an intensity that scared her if she thought about it too much, so she purposely didn't. But every time a text from him hit her phone, it was like she drew a breath for the first time that day.

She met Rachel at a new sushi bar downtown near City Creek. She gave her friend a hug before taking her seat. "It feels like ages since I've seen you."

Rachel grinned, flipping her russet hair over her shoulder. "Time flies when you're busy. Or getting lucky."

"Ugh, just busy right now."

Once they ordered a few rolls and Rachel's beloved mackerel nigiri, Rachel leaned forward. "Catch me up. What's been going on since you started work?"

"Very little, besides work. Travis and I text and sometimes call, but he's as busy as I am at the moment."

"I heard that big shopping center project is falling apart."

Andri nodded. "Yeah, he's really scrambling on it. One of the partners pulled out, but construction is already underway. He has guys that need to be paid and he's worried about the funding collapsing. Neither of us has any time for the other at the moment."

"Well, okay, that sucks...but, things are good, right? You two are working out?"

Andri shrugged, ignoring the twinge, hoping it wouldn't awaken the ache she suffered every night she spent away from him. "We're good. I miss him, though. It sounds like he misses me."

"He does. I saw him yesterday. He looks terrible."

She winced at the thought of Travis suffering. "That doesn't make me feel better."

Rachel ordered a couple more rolls when the waitress stopped by, then said, "I can't tell you how proud I am of myself that I finally got you two together. I knew you'd be good for each other. Someday when you have kids, I can tell them all about how I made sure Mommy and Daddy met."

Andri fumbled her chopsticks. Where had that come from? "Hey, hold on now. You're getting a little ahead of us, don't you think?"

Rachel swallowed a piece of the firecracker roll. "You can't tell me you haven't thought about it."

In truth, she hadn't, not on such a scale, but now that she did, the possibility burst to life in her head and she realized just how easily she could see herself with him. Married. A couple of little dark-haired children running around...and then the darker side. Travis missing out on events with his children because his brother was a mess and needed his help that instant. Travis lashing out as he bowed under the weight of his brother's issues on top of his own family's needs, Andri left to hurt for him but completely unable to relieve him of his burden.

She shivered. "I don't see it getting that far, Rach. I mean, we're great friends, and I really love what we have right now. But unless he can get his need to fix Danny under control...I can't do that again. It was bad enough watching my dad try to fix my mother. I can't go through that with Travis."

"Travis has always assumed too much of everything that happens is either his fault or his responsibility to fix." A shadow crossed Rachel's face and she fell silent for a moment. "Danny will change, Andri. I truly believe that. It won't happen quickly, but it will happen."

"I hope you're right, for both of their sakes." And for her own. Because there was no way she was going to sacrifice her own wellbeing for the long term, and she knew full well that Travis would all too easily sacrifice his.

* * * *

A text hit Travis's phone as he drove on Sunday evening, and when the next light turned red, he glanced at it.

Andri: *Remember, this too shall pass. Miss you.*

He smiled, the warmth that filled him every time he heard from her like the sun welcoming the world from an overly long winter. He missed her like crazy. She was always hovering in the back of his mind, though at night she took center stage in his dreams. The fiery glint in her dark eyes, the sweetness of her mouth, the awareness of her body pressed against his…

He sighed heavily, gripping the steering wheel a little tighter. He'd ruin it. He always failed. The litany turned circles around his thoughts, like engraving on a ring of doom. Jacob, Mother, his marriage, Dan—

No. He shook his head, refusing to add Danny to that list of disasters. He hadn't lost him yet, and he refused to let it happen. And, dammit, he wouldn't add Andri to that list, either.

He wanted her. She'd lifted him, pulled him far enough out of his life's deluge that he could breathe. Part of him screamed warnings. How could he leave himself open to her? Melody had broken his heart. Andri would surely crush his soul. Though he'd just as certainly destroy her first. It was just the way crap worked in his life.

Travis had tried finding a way to shove the idea of Andri into a small box in his head. He'd considered that he should push her back before it was too late for both of them. Count her as a friend, someone fun to be with, someone whose body he thoroughly enjoyed, someone he could talk to. Nothing more.

Aw, who the hell was he kidding? Travis surrendered. He'd wrestled himself and lost, unable to find a way to replace his inner armor without her getting caught inside with him.

No matter how busy he was, thoughts of her always thrummed beneath the surface of whatever other subject occupied him at the moment. The feel of her warm, delicate skin under his fingers simmered in his head when he called his father's physician to make an appointment, Dad arguing every step of the way.

Not that the appointment mattered. Dad had gone home sick again on Thursday, leaving him to juggle the Aspen Terrace center debacle on his own. Damn, he couldn't even get

Dad to the urgent care clinic a mile down the street. He could be such a stubborn old mule sometimes, and Travis failed to find a way to budge him.

He drove to the company offices, promising himself he'd only be there long enough to grab the contracts he'd forgotten when he left a few hours before. Then it was all about Andri. She didn't know he was coming over, but he didn't think she'd mind if he showed up on her doorstep.

He parked, surprised to see his brother's motorcycle there. Why would he be in the office at this time on a Sunday? He let himself in and found Danny by Peggy's desk. A pinprick of concern poked him in the chest. "What are you doing here, Dan?"

His brother looked him square in the eyes. "Nothing much, I've been working on the plans for that new community center at the apartment complex in Herriman. I still feel like I'm playing catch-up half the time."

"Ok, good." Travis couldn't shake the feeling that something was up. Danny was setting off his radar. Now to figure out why. "You still seeing Misty?"

"Oh, hell, no. I haven't seen her since that day you came and got me. She was bad news."

"I thought that was her appeal."

He shrugged, dropping his gaze to the floor. "It was. I'm trying to improve my choices."

"Good. Glad to hear it." Travis stepped away, caught motion in his peripheral vision: Dan sliding his hand into his pocket. A box behind him on the desk drew his eye. The petty cash box. A sick feeling poured through Travis, dark and slimy.

"Dan. Explain that to me."

"Explain what?"

Travis walked over, reached behind him for the box, opened it. It was nearly empty. They always kept two thousand dollars on hand, in case of emergencies, having to pay out a sub quickly, whatever. Anger boiled the fetid stew inside him. "Are you kidding me? I haven't caught you stealing since you were a teenager."

His brother's gaze was impassive. "It's not what you think, Travis."

Travis gritted his teeth, willing himself to hold his temper. "Empty your pockets, Daniel."

Danny sighed heavily and pulled the cash out of his pocket, opened his hand. Travis took it, counted it. "What exactly are you planning on doing with fifteen hundred bucks?"

His brother rolled his eyes. "I don't have to answer to you."

"You're going to have to. Or should I just call the cops?"

Danny's eyes narrowed. "You know, Travis, last I checked, this was a family business. If Dad didn't want me near the petty cash, he wouldn't have shown me where the key is kept."

What was his father thinking? "Dad wouldn't do that."

"Yes, he would. He did."

First, Dad essentially told him to lay off his brother. Now he'd given Danny the keys to the kingdom? "He's a fool to think he can trust you."

Danny's cocky smile warred with the anger darkening his gaze. "I knew you felt that way. Why do you think you know so much more than he does?"

No, this was not going to be about him. This was a Danny issue. "I'm not saying that, I'm just saying that he wants so much to believe in you that he doesn't see you for who and what you are!"

"Ohhh, I see. You know what I am and no one else does, is that it?"

He scrubbed a hand through his hair, determined to calm down. "Dan, you're my brother and I love you. But you're not in a good place."

Danny laughed, but there was no mirth in the harsh sound. "How the fuck would you know?"

Travis flung out a hand toward the box. "Because you're in here stealing from petty cash!"

"God, will you listen to yourself? You have no idea where my head is at right now. You take it upon yourself to be in charge and try to save me, but when was the last time you spent any time with me?" Danny pushed away from the desk, paced a few steps away and then turned back sharply, his finger striking Travis in the chest. "I'm trying to get myself squared away, to figure out who I am. I don't even know, so how the fuck could you know? Oh, wait, that's right, you know better than everyone else. You don't have to really take the time to find out, because you just know."

The attack left Travis confused. "When have you asked me to spend time with you?"

"I finally stopped, oh, about a year ago, because I got tired of you saying no. And that's a two-way-street. When have you *ever* asked me to spend time with you? You're a self-centered prick, Travis."

Travis held his ground, but inside, his gut grew tighter, churning in nauseating twists. He hated the feeling of being wrong. *Failure.*

Danny's temper appeared to have blown itself out when he turned away, then settled on the end of the desk. "Fine, you want an invitation?" he said softly. "Here's one. I'm heading out to a party for my friend, Mara, to say goodbye before she moves to New York for school."

The tension in Travis's chest made him snap. "Yeah, a party with your friends is a great place for a recovering addict."

Danny chuckled, almost under his breath. "God, you won't let it rest for five seconds, will you? Different group of friends, not that I should have to explain it. These are the people who matter, who've stuck by me. Sione Taufua will be there, and he just finished redoing the bathrooms in my townhouse. I owe him money." He pointed at the pile of cash. "Soon as the bank opens tomorrow, I can pull out the cash and return it to the box, like a good boy."

Travis wanted to trust him, but he just couldn't. He'd been lied to so many times. "So where does an invitation fit into all this?"

"Come with me. Come to the party, meet my friends. Maybe if you actually spend some time with me, you'll stop seeing my problems and start seeing me."

Could he be wrong? Could he be so wrapped up in his brother's bouts with addiction that he'd missed him as a person? His heart ached, torn between wanting to go with his brother, keep him safe if the party turned crazy, and the blazing need to see Andri. Damn, he missed her so much even his teeth ached. This fight had wound down, and his craving for Andri ramped up by the minute. "Take the money, Dan. Go have fun."

Dan actually looked a little crestfallen. "You're not coming?"

"I'm not really up for a party. But I want you to promise me that you'll be sober."

"You could play designated driver."

He frowned. "No, Dan. If you're going to get drunk, you shouldn't go at all."

Danny shook his head, a half-smile on his lips. "And here we are, back where we started. Just once I'd like you to be my brother rather than my fucking keeper."

His temper flared and spilled over. "Do you have any idea what I go through for you, Dan? Do you?"

"Don't be a martyr, Travis. I know my problems have bled over onto my family, but you don't have to be that involved. Just be my brother."

"I am being your brother."

"Yeah? Well, you suck at it." Dan gathered the cash, stuffed it in his pocket, and stormed out.

Travis stared at the ceiling for a long while after he heard his brother's motorcycle speed away. His chest ached with stress. The one thing he needed most right now was Andri. He hated asking her to soothe him when she was recovering from her own hellish week, but the fetid slew in the well of his mind had been slowly rising for days. He barely kept his nose above the surface and he was growing tired of treading water. With Andri filling his senses, he'd be able to stop thinking, just float for a while. He hoped that he could fill her needs as well, help her turn off the stress of work and rejuvenate.

He hadn't seen her since he woke up with her Tuesday morning. Would it be too presumptuous to show up at her place and let himself in? She'd given him a key but he hadn't had the chance to use it yet.

He shook his head. Too much whirling around in there, threatening to swamp him. He collected the contracts he came for and left the office.

* * * *

Andri rose from the sofa as a knock on the apartment door sounded. As she crossed the floor, the sound of a key in the lock shot her heart into orbit, followed by a pulsing heat rolling straight to her core. *Travis.*

He let himself in, locked the door, and turned toward her. Darkness and exhaustion shadowed his face, but when he looked at her, the combination of relief and apprehension called to her soul. Her need answered his and she opened her arms to him. Two quick strides and he threw his arms around her, crushing her to him. His mouth sought hers, hot and desperate, tongue tangling with her own, unable to get close enough fast enough.

They tore at their clothes, need pouring over them, leaving them gasping for air and each fighting to hold the other closer, tighter. He lifted her against the wall, his touch finding her ready and wanting. He slid home and everything within her begged for more. He gave her everything she needed, driving her to that kind of relief and renewal only he could provide, and when she cried out and shattered, he followed.

Silence cocooned them as he held her, leaning heavily against her. He shifted back, keeping her in his arms, and made his way to the sofa. He carefully laid her down and settled beside her, arms around her waist, a leg over hers, his head pillowed on her breast. She stroked his hair, reveling in his closeness. It was really ridiculous to have missed him so much, but she couldn't help it.

Something was off, though. While she'd released all the tension she'd carried home from work, he clearly hadn't. She still felt the pressure radiating from his skin. "Think you might share what's got you so tied up in knots, Travis?"

Silence answered her for a moment, then he said, "You're good at that."

"What?"

"Seeing what's going on in my head."

"Not hard tonight. So what's bothering you?"

He groaned. "I'm sorry, Andri. I didn't want to carry this in here with me."

She kissed his hair. "Don't worry about it. Talk to me."

"It's Daniel. We had a fight before I came over."

"Well, that explains a lot." As hard, hot, and fast as they'd gone at each other, there had to be more than general frustration driving it.

"I caught him taking money from petty cash. He said it was to pay a guy who did some work for him, but how can I know for sure? It wouldn't be the first time he swiped money for drugs."

Yikes. That had to hurt. "Do you think he's relapsed?"

He propped himself up on his elbow and looked at her. "I don't know. I mean, the usual signs aren't there, but still, how do I know? I'm so worried about him, and he ended up mad at me for judging him."

She drew a finger along his forehead, down his cheek. "If he is clean, I can see where he would feel that way."

His brow knitted, frustration filling his eyes. "I hate that you do that, sometimes."

"What?"

"See both sides of things, like a referee. You're supposed to be on my side."

She caressed his jaw. "I am. I'm trying to help you navigate this."

Travis turned his face into her palm, pressing a kiss to her flesh. "He invited me to go to a party tonight, meet his friends. Supposedly his good friends as opposed to his druggie crowd."

"Why didn't you?"

He frowned. "I wanted to be with you."

She smiled a little. Did he have any idea how he tugged at her heart? "I'd have still been here, Travis. Do you spend any time with him, really, or is it all about his problems?"

Tension rippled over his frame. "I'm not a bad brother, Andri."

"I didn't say that. I said, maybe you do need to spend time with him, and try to ignore everything that's come before." She sat up when he did and placed a hand on his shoulder. "Look, I'm not saying that's easy. It takes monumental effort for me, just talking to my mother on the phone, to focus on how she is now instead of who she was for most of my life. Instinctively, I expect the monster every single time. And sometimes I get it, even now. For my dad, it wasn't until the end of his life that he realized he'd been so focused on trying to save her that he'd stopped treating her like the love of his life. There was so little left of their relationship."

Travis turned away from her and scrubbed his hand through his hair. "Damn, I can't win tonight." He stood and reached for his clothes, yanking them on.

She cringed inside at the anger etched in his expression. Why did she always do that? She'd never learned how to be quiet when she should, preserving someone's feelings rather than pushing forward in an effort to help. Now she'd pushed too hard. "Travis."

He thrust his foot into a shoe and pulled his car keys from his pocket, looking disheveled and beyond frustrated. "Andri, I have given everything I have to take care of Danny and protect him, and suddenly everyone is telling me I've done it wrong. I already know I'm a failure, I don't need everyone else piling on."

She rose, but resisted the urge to crowd him. He raised his palm to her, freezing her in place. "Listen, I can't do this tonight. I'm angry, and frustrated, and if I don't leave now, I'm going to say something I'll regret."

She crossed her arms over her middle, nodding. He closed the door softly behind him and she let out a heavy sigh. She hated where his head was, but she knew why he was there. What killed her was not knowing how to pull him out of such a vicious cycle. He alone could do that.

She took a fast shower, then lay in bed, staring at the ceiling in the dark. Her people skills could only take her so far, and her man skills clearly didn't extend this far. Her experiences with an addict, the things she had learned, weren't the only path to survival, but they were all she had to offer to Travis, to help him in his struggle. Yet, she dreaded the feeling that she was troubleshooting in the dark. She had no idea what to do, going forward, aside from somehow learning to bite her tongue when tempted to give advice.

Good thing she was working again. She found comfort in the world of networks and hardware and software. Those concrete things she understood. Even when something was glitchy in her work world, it was always something built in, something tangible that she could find and fix. People on the other hand...even when she could pinpoint the problem, she couldn't just swap in a replacement chip or board. Travis would have to fix himself or remain forever tortured.

Why did that nugget of reality have to hurt so much?

Chapter Eleven

Travis sat in the truck after leaving Andri, waiting for the traffic light to change. He hated how he felt, and even worse, he hated that he'd lashed out at Andri. What the hell was wrong with him? Was he trying to push her away? He should be listening to her advice. She'd been there. But his stubborn refusal to fail tripped him up, again and again.

He called before he hit Parley's Canyon.

"Hi." Andri sounded reserved. Cool. What did he expect?

"Hey. Thanks for picking up. I half expected to be groveling on voice mail."

"I much prefer to receive groveling via live connection. In person is best, but I'll take it over the phone."

He took the next exit, driving back under the interstate so he could return to the valley. Going home wasn't an option. He knew where he needed to be. "I have no excuses for lashing out at you. I'm so sorry, sweetheart."

He waited for a second, then, hastily added, "Let me do that again as soon as I can get back to you. I'll apologize properly, at your feet. I'll beg forgiveness on my knees. I'll do it at your door if you don't want to let me in."

She sighed. "Travis. You've apologized. It's okay."

"Yeah, but it was a phone apology. Lame."

"Could've been worse. You could have texted."

That made him chuckle in spite of himself, but it was a momentary respite. "Is it okay if I come back to you tonight? I'll do whatever you want me to."

She sighed. "Travis. You're forgiven. Come home to me."

When she disconnected, he turned his attention to the road, determined to reach her as quickly as he could without being pulled over. This had to stop. He was pushing his luck with her. One of these days, she'd hit breaking point with his attitude, and then she'd be gone for good. He wouldn't blame her. In fact, he'd have no one but himself to blame, and wasn't that exactly what he was trying to avoid in the first place? He cursed. He was damned if he did and damned if he didn't. But for now, for tonight, she was waiting for him. He shut down his thoughts and drove.

* * * *

Travis had been a workaholic since his divorce, and he'd watched Andri put in her share of killer days. In an effort to strengthen what he had with her, Travis made a point of cutting back on the overtime as much as he could over the next couple of weeks to spend time with her. She trimmed her own schedule in return.

One Thursday night, Travis found himself desperately trying to beat Andri on the new first-person-shooter game she'd picked up. Unfortunately, she was a terror with a game controller in her hands and she was kicking his ass.

She was closing in for the kill when her newly adopted gray cat, Fluffball, ripped around the corner of the sofa and pounced on Andri's bare feet. She shrieked, and Travis took advantage of the distraction of kitty claws and blasted her avatar on screen. "Yes! Nice timing, Fluff."

Andri shooed the cat away and gave him a dirty look, though the sparkle in her eyes dampened the effect. "You and the cat are ganging up on me. That's terrific."

The cat chose that moment to jump up on Travis's lap and rub his head against his forearm. He scratched Fluffball's ears. "Guys have to stick together, especially when a girl is beating one of them at a game she shouldn't be good at."

Her brows lifted. "That I shouldn't be good at? Why, because I'm a girl?"

"Anything I say to that is going to be wrong, isn't it?"

"Probably. Might want to stop while you're ahead. Best two out of three?"

"You're on." His phone rang, startling the cat off his lap. He fished the phone out of his pocket, cursed under his breath, then answered. "Hey, Dan. What's up?"

"Trav, uh, hey. Are you busy?" His voice sent a tremor through Travis's gut. He knew that low, not-quite-normal tone, the slight slur in his words.

"Damn you, Daniel. You're drunk."

"Um, not entirely. Couple other things all mixed in there too. Listen, I'm kind of in trouble and I need you."

Andri placed a hand on his thigh, her expression rich with concern. He covered her fingers with his, siphoning strength. "What's going on? Where are you?"

"I was hanging out with a couple of guys, and more people showed up, and it got outta hand. And I did some stuff, so that was kind of fucked-up, but I could be way more wasted, so that's good, right?"

"Yeah, that's a huge improvement. Just a little wasted instead of completely." He cringed at the cruel edge in his tone, but at the same time, it was all coming to a head now, frustration rushing up from the cauldron deep inside him, threatening to cut off his voice, cut off his air, force him under the torrent. "What do you want from me, Dan?"

"We took a little roadie, so now I'm—oh, where the fuck are we? Oh, yeah. Wendover. I'm broke and I could use some cash. 'Cause, you know, we got a room, but I want to hit the buffet and I think Korbin's car's out of gas so that makes getting home tomorrow…oh. Hey, so I'm stuck, I guess. I didn't drive and that's a really good thing because I am way not safe on the road right now, but I swear to God, if you get me some cash, I won't even play roulette. Except I might win, so I could pay you back and then some, right?"

When Travis didn't respond, Danny said, "Please? Come on, hook me up, Trav." Someone in the background mumbled something and Danny laughed. "Yeah, hey, don't sit there doing the pissed off big bro thing. Cut me some slack or I'm gonna be stuck out here."

God, he was so tired, exhausted deep down to the tattered, dark pit where his threadbare soul huddled against the cold, raging sea. He looked into Andri's eyes, seeking comfort. As long as he kept giving Danny everything he wanted, when he wanted it, he was never going to learn to take care of himself. "Danny, you cannot be serious. Why do you think I'll bail you out of this little adventure?"

What was it that he'd promised himself? When it happened again, he'd send his father. Yes, that was the answer. "Do you have Dad's cell number?"

Danny swore. "Trav, oh, man, please, I don't want to talk to Dad right now. Come on, it's not like I'm asking all that much. Fifty bucks will get me fed and home tomorrow, and I won't even gamble it. I'll do anything you want."

"No. Call Dad."

Silence stretched over the phone for a moment before Danny cleared his throat. "I can't. I don't want him to hate me."

That stung, fierce and hot, like a stab from a monster wasp. He heard all too clearly what Danny meant—*I don't want him to hate me like you do, Travis.* "Look, Dan, it'll be okay. Just call dad. It'll be fine. Call him before it gets any later. I'll talk to you over the weekend."

He disconnected the call, setting his phone on the arm of the sofa. He leaned into Andri after she placed her game controller on the table. "Tell me I did the right thing."

She wrapped her arms around him. "*Kardia mou.* My heart. Everything will be okay." He chose to let himself believe her. And for that night, making love to her and then sleeping curled around her, cocooned together in her bed with Fluffball sprawled along the bottom of the mattress near Andri's feet, for that capsule of time, everything was just fine.

Andri had an early meeting, so she left him in bed with Fluffball draped over his legs. He listened to the soft sounds of the world waking up after she closed the door. The cat's gentle purr combined with the birds in the trees outside the window in a natural lullaby, and he thought perhaps he could drift back to sleep for an hour. He turned, pulling Andri's pillow to his chest, tucking it under his chin. It carried traces of her scent, vanilla and woman, and it comforted him.

Strange how much a part of him she'd become, like a missing piece of his puzzle had finally been fitted into place. His own shortcomings were blessedly silent and the sense of peace rejuvenated him. Not enough to go back to sleep, though, so he gave up and hit the shower. He stood at the foot of Andri's bed, toweling off, when his phone rang.

"Travis?" A shimmering thread of terror wove through his mother's voice, hitting his gut like a shot. "I don't know what to do. I came down to his office, he's on the floor—"

Dad. His blood turned to ice. "Did you call the paramedics?"

"No, no, Travis, please, I can't do this, oh, God, I can't lose him, too!"

Memories rose of Jacob, of that terrible moment when his parents forced open the bathroom door. He gritted his teeth, pushing the phantoms back. He had to focus. "Mother, I'll call them, I'll meet you at the hospital." He hung up, realizing she wasn't listening. She'd dissolved into hysteria.

Fear gutted him, leaving his fingers trembling. Travis yanked a black t-shirt over his head, then grabbed his wireless headset from the kitchen counter and hooked it over his ear. He dialed for emergency assistance, giving his parents' address to the dispatcher as he pulled on his jeans, socks, and boots, then clipped the phone to his belt. He stayed on with the dispatcher as he drove, until the paramedics reached his parents' home and relayed that his father was alive, and his frantic mother would travel with them to the medical center.

After the dispatcher hung up, Travis tightened his fists around the steering wheel, searching inside for a way to stave off the panic churning through his system. He refocused himself on anger, a tool he could use to stay sharp. He cursed his father for putting off seeing his physician. He cursed himself. Damn, why hadn't he just taken Dad to his appointment? And what if those moments lost when his mother called him rather than emergency assistance were too precious, the moments dividing a chance at life from certain death?

He refocused again, ordering the logical part of his brain to override the growing fear chilling him from the inside out. There would be paperwork to fill out. Clearly his mother would be in no condition to handle any of those details. And where did Dan fit in all this? Where was he?

An image of Andri slipped forward into his line of thought, a picture of her wrapping her arms around him. The need for her caught like a spark on tinder, flaring, licking along the edge of the growing fear for his father. He'd give anything to crawl into bed with her and block everything else out. But there was too much resting on his shoulders to escape now.

He clenched his jaw, thrusting everything back to the depths inside him. He had to get through whatever lay ahead with his father. He had to take care of his mother, whether she wanted him to or not. He had to track down his brother and get him back on the road to recovery. He'd handle the business via cell phone.

Everything would be fine.

It had to be.

Travis refused to consider any other possibility.

Chapter Twelve

The accountant with the printing problem breathed a huge sigh of relief through the phone at Andri. She silently thanked her lucky stars at the sound of the printer pulling in paper. She closed out the error report on her screen as she said goodbye to the woman on the line. Crisis averted.

She picked up her cell, which had vibrated against her hip three times while she handled the epic printing disaster. Rachel. Must be important. Rachel picked up on the first ring.

"Andri. Have you talked to Travis?" She could hear the van rumbling in the background. Rachel was on the road.

"Not since I left for work, why?" A foreboding shiver ran down her spine.

Rachel cursed at another driver. "Peggy, the office manager, called me. His dad's in the hospital."

Oh, no. "What happened?"

"Heart attack."

The bottom dropped out of her day. *Oh, Travis,* kardia mou. "Which hospital?"

"That big one in Murray. I'm on my way to Danny's place to let him know. Brat's not answering his phone."

"I'll get up there as soon as I can." Andri disconnected, grabbed her purse, and hurried to her assistant's desk.

Shalyndra looked up as she reached the desk. "What's up, boss?"

"I've got to take off." She glanced at the clock on the desk. "Call it an early lunch, and I will probably be gone a couple of hours. Think you and Chen can shoulder the load?"

"Sure. Everything okay?"

"I don't know. My boyfriend's dad is in the hospital. I'll check in with you in an hour."

Andri tapped the button for the elevator, silently cheering when the doors slid open immediately. She stepped in, then groaned as the elevator ignored her basement level request and moved up a floor to the executive level, the need of someone above her apparently more important to the elevator than getting her to the parking garage. She clamped down on her frustration as the door slid open and GlobalTech's tall, blond CEO, Jamie Mickleson, joined her in the elevator. He smiled down at her as the elevator finally moved in the right direction.

"Hello, Andri. I haven't had a chance to stop in and check on you, but I'm hearing good things."

She flashed a quick smile. "Thank you."

"So, what do you think of GlobalTech? How are you getting along here?"

Distracted, silently cursing each dragging minute that kept her from getting to Travis, she realized he'd asked a question a beat too late. She blurted out, "I love it, thanks for the opportunity."

His brow knitted, concern shadowing his features. "You sure? Is there a problem?"

Andri clenched her shaking hands, knowing her anxiety must be written on her face. As the boss, Mr. Mickleson would naturally interpret it as work issues. Ugh, damage control. "No, really, work is fantastic. I'm just, um…personal issues. Don't mind me."

"Do you need to take the day off?"

She'd only been there a month, taking time off would look even flakier than stealing a long lunch. "It's okay. I might be extra long at lunch today, though. My boyfriend's dad had a heart attack this morning—"

Mickleson held up a large hand. "The hours you're putting in haven't escaped my notice. If you need time, take it. Anything your team can't handle will wait. Get out of here."

She already loved working there, but that won her undying loyalty. "You're the best. I'll be in tomorrow."

The doors opened on the second floor, her boss's destination, and as he stepped out, he said, "Tomorrow is Saturday. I don't want to hear that you came in over the weekend."

She nodded as the doors slid closed.

Worry filled every cell of her body, pulsing with her heartbeat as she reached her car. She found herself praying, a mantra pleading for a good outcome repeating through her mind as she drove. She exited the interstate and worked her way into the chain of parking lots surrounding the massive medical center, her heart aching for the fear and stress Travis must be under. It suddenly felt far longer than a few hours since she'd last seen him. Never in her life had Andri stood by and let someone she cared for suffer alone. No power on earth could make her start now.

She snagged a parking spot as an older couple pulled out. She ran all the way to the information desk, where she was directed to the waiting room nearest the intensive care unit.

The antiseptic scent in the climate-controlled air flooded her with memories of visiting her father in the hospital, during that last few weeks before the doctors recommended hospice care at home. *We'll make the last of his time as painless as we can,* the oncologist had said. *Let him go with dignity, surrounded by your love.*

Her breath caught when she spotted Travis. He sat on a chair in the waiting room, elbows on his knees, his head in his hands. She walked over to him, stood before him.

"Travis." When he didn't respond, she knelt before him and reached between his arms, laying a hand on either side of his face. He jumped when she touched him and jerked his head up. Her heart slammed to a halt at the deep agony in his eyes, and she wondered for a split second how he could still function with all that bottled up inside him. *How much more can you stuff behind that wall, Travis?*

Thought fled, the need to hold him overwhelming her. She slid between his legs and folded her arms across his hard, muscled back. He crushed the air from her lungs when he pulled her to him with one arm, his other hand clutching her hair, his face buried against her neck.

She held him until her knees complained about the hard floor beneath them. She gently disengaged herself from his hold and stood up, her joints, and her heart, protesting every inch of the way. She whispered, "How's he doing, Travis?"

"He's in surgery. I'm sure he'll be fine." The cold detachment in his voice shook her. Travis put his hands on her hips and shifted her away from him, then stood up. "How did you find out about this?"

"Rachel called me after she got the news from the office."

He nodded and pulled his cell phone from his belt and scrolled through contact numbers. "I should call the rest of the relatives. Uncle Mac and Aunt Sarah are over in the emergency room with Mother. She had a full-blown panic attack after Dad went into surgery."

Travis looked around, apparently registering the presence of other people in the waiting room. He looked down at Andri with a long, hard look she couldn't decipher, then twined his fingers through hers and led her back to the elevator. Outside the hospital, Andri sat on a bench and alternated between watching the clouds roll across the sky above the Salt Lake valley, gathering for a storm, and watching Travis pace.

He called several relatives, his calm, collected business voice taking him through the repetition of basic details on each call. His dad had gone to pick up Danny in Wendover. Only to Andri did Travis mention his dad's decision to retrieve his son rather than send him the money he'd wanted. He'd taken Danny home, returned to his own home, and had a bad few hours trying to sleep. Sophia had found him in the morning, on his office floor.

After a while, Travis stood staring at the phone in his hand. A hint of panic flickered across his face before he crammed it back again. "That takes care of family," he said softly. He dialed again, this time carrying on a conversation with one of his construction supervisors about the status on certain projects. By the time he made his third business call, Andri's frustration hummed under her skin. How could the man work at a time like this?

As he scanned through his contact list yet again, Andri stood and grabbed his hand. "What are you doing, Travis? I'm sure everyone will understand if work comes to a screeching halt for a while."

His walled gaze met hers. "It's business, Andri. I'm the head of the company while Dad's out of commission, and I have responsibilities of my own, in addition to taking on his. I can't just walk away because I feel damned miserable at the moment."

Andri shook her head, frustration building. "Travis, you have to stop. Seriously."

"I don't need—"

She stopped him with a finger on his lips, not attempting to bank the anger in her voice. "Don't even say it. Don't tell me you don't need my help. I know, you're a freaking machine. You can handle everything all alone and remain stoic through it all. But, Travis, I love you. You're holding the weight of the world, you're stressed and afraid, and watching you refuse to acknowledge it is killing me. I'm going to help whether you like it or not."

She didn't mean to say she loved him, but it had come out in such a rush, perhaps he didn't notice. He stared at her, the storm brewing in his eyes a reflection of the storm gathering over their heads. "Andri, I—" He broke off, his voice rough. He cleared his throat. "I appreciate you for coming, I really do. But I have to work right now."

"No, you don't." Andri took the cell phone out of his hand and clipped it onto his belt. She grasped both his hands in hers, giving him a good squeeze. "No more work today, Travis. Everyone will understand."

Something slipped a little behind his gaze. Work, Travis's favorite escape mechanism. She'd removed it, and she knew he recognized that he wasn't getting it back. Travis shook his head and pulled her close to him. *Round one, Andri.* She walked by his side back to Intensive Care.

Sophia Holt stood in the middle of the waiting room when they arrived. Travis went to his mother, cradling her shoulders in his arm, steadying her. Sophia let him support her for a moment, until her gaze landed on Andri. Sophia stiffened and laid a slim hand on Travis's chest, pushing him away. She hoped with every fiber of her being that Sophia wasn't angry with Travis because she was there. It would be just her luck to cause a greater strain on Travis's relationship with his mother.

Sophia turned and walked away from her son, settling into a chair beside another woman who closely resembled her. Her sister, perhaps. The anger and hurt raking across Travis's hard features cut Andri to the quick. She took his hand, and he led her to a chair.

One hour eased into two. The tension cranked up with each tick of the waiting room clock. Andri curled up on the chair, observing the way Travis's family interacted. She learned a great deal, most of which saddened her. Terrence's sister, Sarah, stayed by Sophia's side, along with Sophia's sister, Francesca. The women held her hands. Francesca spoke quietly. "Let's go to the cafeteria, Sophie. You need to eat something, honey, to keep up your strength."

Sarah nodded. "At least come with us for coffee."

Sophia shook her head, eyes red but dry. "I can't," she said, her voice thin.

Francesca looked over at Travis, pleading in her eyes, and Andri felt him tense up and scoot to the edge of his seat, ready to serve his mother in any way she'd allow him.

"How about I send Travis for something," his aunt said. "Even a croissant or an apple would help."

Sophia glanced in her son's direction and shook her head again. "No. Maybe some coffee. Would you mind getting some, Sarah?"

Andri watched Travis as his mother shut down the invitation for him to help. His expression darkened for a split second before clearing. How much practice must he have had to be able to show so little reaction to being dismissed by his own mother? His aunts doted on his mother, shored her up, doing all those things Andri knew Travis would do, if only Sophia let him. Instead, the woman shut her son out. It bewildered her.

Terrence's brother Mac, and his wife, Deanna, brought a jigsaw puzzle to the hospital, and slowly assembled a photograph of the Manhattan skyline on a table in the waiting room. Mac spoke to Travis briefly, and Deanna hugged him and patted him on the cheek, telling him everything would be fine, people survived worse things every day. Travis, calm as ever, thanked them, asked them if they needed anything. Finally, Travis cut himself away from everyone and stood at the window.

Andri went to him when it became clear he intended to stay where he was. She stood beside him, watching the heavy storm clouds release their loads of rain. She ran her hand down Travis's arm, reading his stress in his taut muscles.

She kept her voice quiet for the sake of what little privacy the big room offered. "Travis, are you hungry? Do you want something to drink?"

He matched her soft volume, not returning her gaze. "No."

Lifting a hand, she started rubbing the muscles at the back of his neck. He winced before he shrugged her hand away. "Don't," he said.

"You have a headache."

"I'm fine."

"Yeah, I'm sure you are. And I'm also sure you have a headache that could knock over a horse." She grabbed his hand and tugged him to follow her, which he reluctantly did. He dropped onto a sofa, and she settled in behind him, her legs to either side of his. She leaned up close to his ear. "I know it sounds ridiculous, under the circumstances, but try to relax."

He took a deep breath, held it for a moment, then exhaled as she put her hands to work on his neck and shoulders. She kneaded his muscles, not quite easing the tension from him before he tightened up again. She spoke quietly to him while she worked his shoulders. "Travis, don't fight me. Concentrate on my touch, don't think about anything else."

After a few minutes, he let his head drop slightly, then her efforts started working. She blocked out all thought, concentrating on his steel shoulders. She massaged the width of his shoulders, down his back between his shoulder blades, up the sides of his neck to the base of his skull.

When his muscles felt sufficiently relaxed, Andri slid her hands down past his collarbone and pressed against his chest. He shifted forward in the sofa and leaned back against her. She laid her fingers against his temples, rubbing in gentle circles. "Close your eyes, Travis."

He obeyed, and she studied his thick brown lashes for a moment before returning to her self-appointed task. She massaged across his scalp, along his jaw, behind his ears. He suddenly felt heavier against her, as if the tension had vanished, and she smiled, triumphant. She'd put him to sleep. She leaned her head against the back of the sofa, stroking his hair. His weight settled against her felt so comfortable, so right. She draped her arms across his chest and just before Andri closed her eyes, she caught a glance from Travis's uncle. Mac smiled at her, relief in his expression, then returned his attention to the puzzle.

Andri drifted in the netherworld between sleep and full consciousness, not knowing or caring how much time passed. All that mattered was her awareness of Travis's body covering hers, the intimacy of him sleeping in her arms. He stirred, jogging her back to alertness when he sat up slightly and turned to look at her. She opened her eyes, finding a hint of peace in Travis's gaze. A peace that vanished when someone appeared in the doorway. Travis shifted away from her as Rachel walked in. Danny followed, his hair damp from the storm and plastered against his face and neck.

Emotions warred within Andri as she observed Danny. He was unshaven, eyes bloodshot, but his clothes were clean. Maybe Rachel made him shower before coming over, to make him more presentable for the family. Sometimes her dad had done that with Ma. More often than not, he took Andri and Dmitri to whatever event had arrived and made excuses for her mother's absence.

Other than a few glances at the rest of the family, Danny kept his eyes on the ground. His shoulders slumped forward and remorse radiated from him. She didn't know him well at all, yet Andri wasn't sure which emotion carved deeper into her heart: anger at what he put Travis through, or sorrow for Danny's continued war with his demons.

Danny walked over to his mother. She patted his hand before returning her attention to her sister. His shoulders rounded in further and he shuffled over and dropped into a chair beside the sofa. Rachel took the next chair.

Travis grabbed Andri's hand, weaving his fingers between hers, his grip hard, as if he were holding on for dear life. "Thanks for bringing him, Rachel."

Rachel nodded and Danny looked up at Travis. The stark anguish in his expression startled Andri. His throat worked for a moment. "How is he, Trav?"

"We don't know yet. He's—" Travis abruptly stopped and surged to his feet, pulling Andri up with him, as a doctor entered the waiting room.

Sophia rose, a white-knuckled grip on her sister and sister-in-law. "Dr. Stone," she said, a tremor in her voice. "How is my husband?"

"Mrs. Holt. He's back in the ICU. The damage was extensive. I'm afraid I can't make any promises."

Andri released Travis when Danny's eyes squeezed closed, his face contorted in pain. Travis put an arm around his brother, whispering comfort. She rose to stand by Rachel, whose red eyes and hitching breath betrayed her fears. "Hey, you okay, Rach?"

She nodded, reaching for a tissue on a nearby table and wiping her nose. "Yeah. Terry's like a second dad," Rachel whispered. "I love him so much, and I'm scared."

Andri hugged her dear friend close. What could she say? It will be okay? No. Because every person in the room who cared about Terrence Holt knew it very well might not be okay, ever again.

The rest of the day passed with unbearable sluggishness. Travis tried to care for his family, especially his mother, throughout the day. Sophia was polite, but completely withdrawn from her sons. Danny didn't bother to try engaging her. Travis never gave up trying. He attempted to reach her, bringing whatever she might need. He reached for her in more subtle ways, too. A touch on her shoulder, a gentle squeeze of her hand, but she pushed him away, sometimes literally.

When Andri looked in Travis's eyes, she saw the wall, higher and thicker than ever, blocking his emotions. She sighed, her heart heavy at the exposure of so much of Travis's baggage. She watched him cater to everyone's needs while she turned the situation over in her head, putting the pieces into place. She'd bet money that there was a correlation between his mother and his ex. Had Travis married a woman too much like his mother, still seeking approval, and finding more of the same? That would explain why he retreated sometimes, closing himself off from her. It would also go a long way toward explaining why Travis believed he was such a failure in his relationships and other areas of his life.

What a mess. How would he ever fully trust her and give her his heart when this is what he knew?

* * * *

It took Travis all damned day, but he finally managed to shut his emotions down completely. He had to, if he wanted to function at all. And function he must. His mother needed so much more than what he had to offer, but he could still make sure she had comfort, even if his part of providing it meant ensuring she was surrounded by people whose help she would accept. To facilitate that, he took care of his aunts and uncles who came and went as the hours passed. He fetched coffee, water, snacks, anything he could do to be helpful.

Danny had shut down too. He hadn't stayed long. After the doctor's report, he took time to see Dad. When his brother walked out, the anxiety emblazoned on his face made Travis embrace him. Yeah, his little brother was a mess, but he read him well enough to know he felt responsible for Dad. The litany in Travis's head had already added his father to his personal failure list, so he knew too well how Danny felt. Neither he nor Danny, apparently, could find words to fill the space between them. He was grateful when Rachel took his brother home.

When the day had given way to night and most of the local relatives had drifted back home to wait for further developments, Travis entered his father's room. The sight of his vibrant, larger than life figure lying helpless in the hospital bed nearly drove him to his knees.

A respirator helped his dad breathe, and Travis stared at the readings on the monitors for a long time, finding comfort in the steady blips and stable numbers on the display. Finally, he reached out and closed his hand around his father's. When had his hand grown larger than Dad's? So many memories as a child, placing their palms together, wondering if his little fingers would ever be the same size. Now it had happened and he didn't remember when.

"Dad," he whispered, tears threatening to choke his ability to speak entirely. "Please fight. You have to get better."

He touched his father's face, stroked his hair. "I'm not...I don't know if I'll ever be the man you are. You're so damned strong. I try to emulate you, but an imitation is the best I can do, and it's a pale one. Please get better. Please, Daddy."

He swiped his sleeve across his eyes, wiping up the tears he couldn't control. He leaned down and pressed his lips to his father's pale forehead. "I don't know how to carry everything by myself, but I will do it. I'll find a way. I'll take care of Mother and Danny. The company. I'll hold it all until you're better, I promise. You don't have to worry about anything but healing."

A knock at the door preceded a nurse stepping in to check his father. He nodded at her, squeezed his father's hand one more time, then left the room.

When he returned to the waiting room, Andri, concern emanating from her frame, wrapped her arms around him. He let her embrace him until her gentle comfort threatened to shatter his ability to hold everything together. He stepped back, grabbing her hands and kissing them, trying to let her know he appreciated her without losing it.

"You should get some sleep," she said, trailing her fingers down his cheek, her touch cracking his heart around the edges. "Let me take you home."

He shook his head. "I need to stay with my mother. Please understand."

Her smile seemed sad. "I do, *kardia mou*."

He kissed her. He wanted her to stay with everything he had, but he had nothing to offer her in return. Not right now. And that was hardly fair. "Go home, sweetheart. Sleep. Give Fluffball some attention."

She looked at him for a long moment, clearly sifting and weighing her options. Finally, she nodded. "If you need anything, I don't care what time it is, you call. Promise me."

"I promise."

Chapter Thirteen

Travis left the hospital at two in the morning, because his mother demanded it. Additional aunts, uncles, and cousins would be arriving over the next few hours, and someone had to be at his parents' house to let them in and get them settled. At least she'd finally asked something of him. That was a step in the right direction.

He caught sleep in patches, in between those moments when he jerked awake and had to re-orient himself, remembering where he was, and those when the doorbell rang and more of the family arrived.

The phone woke him again at seven in the morning. "Travis." It was Uncle Mac, and the tremor in his voice sent an answering quake through his gut. "I'm bringing your mother home."

"Dad?"

Mac's voice broke. "Another heart attack, about an hour ago. He's gone."

The world spun wrong, and he sank to his knees, fighting for breath, the phone slipping from his fingers. In the distance, he heard someone crying out in agony. It took a few moments to register it was his own voice.

He pulled himself to his feet. His heart shredded, flaking apart, every fiber of his being aching. He couldn't take it anymore. It was too much. Far, far too much.

Andri. Her image swam in his mind, an oasis taunting him as he stood, shaking, in the hellish wasteland of his life. He'd crawl, broken and bleeding to where she was, but what if she vanished, like a mirage?

He was vaguely aware of an aunt and uncle entering the room. His mouth moved on autopilot, sharing the news. More crying, clinging to each other, reaching for him—

No. Need for Andri forced him out the door. He concentrated harder than he ever had in his life to drive safely, blocking out everything but her. He clawed every last ounce of strength he had left from the tattered wisps of his soul, forced it into focus. He had to get to Andri.

She opened the apartment door as he fitted the key in the lock. She stepped back as he stumbled through.

"Travis, what's wrong?"

He shook his head and she took his hand, drawing him to the sofa. He sank onto it. Instantly, she crouched beside him, her arms pulling him to her. It shattered him. "He's gone, Andri," he whispered, the last of his strength fleeing. "My dad died."

"Oh, Travis. *Kardia mou*, I'm so sorry." She wrapped herself around him, arms and legs. He tightened his arms around her, and the overwhelming feeling of security crushed the broken pieces of him into powder, scattering him like autumn leaves in the wind. He tucked his face into her neck as tears streamed down his cheeks. The pain ripped through him, and he cried out. He clung to her, shaking, as everything he'd stuffed into the dark corners of his soul poured out of him.

Andri rocked him, her own tears coursing down her face in response to his agony. There were no words of comfort, nothing at all she could say. She recalled her own loss, the depth of that pain, knowing that his must surely be worse. At least she had known her loss was coming. She'd had time to bleed out the misery over the weeks before her dad breathed his last. Travis's burst all at once.

She did the only thing she could. She held him and let him mourn.

When his brutal storm of emotion finally subsided, Travis pressed a kiss to her throat before shifting away from her. She let him go, watching him walk down the hall to the bathroom. He moved slowly, gingerly, as though every muscle in his body ached.

Andri heard the shower running and went to make him a sandwich, though she suspected his stomach was too tied in knots to eat it. Travis walked into the kitchen a few minutes later, his hair still damp. He'd changed into a gray t-shirt and black jeans he'd left in the drawer she'd cleared out for him.

He slid an arm around her shoulders and kissed her temple. "Thank you." His voice was gruff, raw. He stepped back as she reached for him. "I should go. I'm sure there will be a lot to do, and I'm the one who has to do it."

"Did you get any sleep last night?" She guessed by the smudges under his eyes that he hadn't.

Travis gave her a non-committal shrug that she was pretty sure meant *not really*. "I will at some point." He looked down at her, his gaze unreadable. "You're going to be the most stable person in my life for the next little while. And I don't know what in the hell I'm supposed to do exactly. Would you mind helping me?"

She swallowed hard, determined not to get teary-eyed on him, though his request tugged hard on her compassion. As if he needed to ask. "Of course."

* * * *

Over the next several days, Travis remained subdued, very clearly functioning by sheer force of will. His mother had completely fallen apart and Danny wasn't in any better shape, so Andri provided assistance everywhere she could as Travis worked out the details of his father's funeral and burial.

The time passed in a blur of planning and coping with paperwork. Andri split her time between work, where her team and her boss offered incredible support, and being with Travis, shoring him up however she could. She felt incredible gratitude for Travis's brilliant office manager, who took nearly all his company obligations off his shoulders. She'd see to it that Travis sent the woman on a vacation when everything eventually settled to what would be the new normal.

She sat with Travis at his father's desk while he sorted through Terrence's day to day life, making sure any bills were paid. He paused when he uncovered some pamphlets. "What is this?"

Andri stood beside him, looking over his shoulder as he perused the information before him. The pamphlets came from a local support group for addicts and their families, similar to the one she and Dmitri had attended in Colorado. Travis set the pamphlets aside and picked up another sheet, printed with meeting times and locations. Tuesday and Thursday evening meetings stood out, circled in red pen.

Travis dropped the paper on the desk and sat back in the chair. Confusion flickered in the dark depths of his gaze. "I wonder if Dad went to those meetings."

"Maybe. Do you think your mom went with him?"

He shook his head. "I'd like to think so. If either of them did, maybe they've already learned some of what you've tried to explain to me. I'd sure feel better if Dad died with a little peace where Danny is concerned."

Andri wondered if Danny had attended any meetings. If he had, maybe things were getting better, little by little, and Travis wasn't seeing it. Though a backslide like the one that took his brother to Wendover probably damaged his optimism.

The funeral service was huge. It was held at a church in the Holts' neighborhood, and the building filled to overflowing. Terrence had lived a full, generous, respected life, and it seemed everyone who had ever met him, even the most passing of acquaintances, came to mourn his death. Andri sat beside Travis, glancing back a row at Rachel, Ian, and their parents, who had flown in to pay their respects. Those who spoke, including Travis and two of Terrence's siblings, related fun times and memories of him. Still, a feeling of deep, abiding sadness clouded the building.

Andri measured the sharp contrast to the party they'd had for her father. Again, perhaps, the mood varied so drastically because they'd had time to prepare. Dad had insisted that he didn't want sadness, he wanted joy. So they threw a party. Friends and family alike swapped stories and laughed for hours. They had even decorated his gravesite with balloons and party favors in addition to flowers.

Ma had been sober, just for Dad, and in giving it everything she had to remember only the happiness, it helped her start to heal and truly desire to be different. That had been her starting point, though it took both Andri and Dmitri refusing to play her games or cater to her to finally make Ma turn around for good.

Andri looked over at Danny, slumped on the pew, hair hanging in his face. She knew suffering such a great loss could easily send him over a cliff. But maybe it would do the opposite. Maybe it would push him in a better direction. Andri prayed it would. She kept her thoughts to herself, though, knowing what a touchy issue it was for Travis. If things were really getting better, eventually he would realize it for himself.

After the graveside service, people crowded around Travis and his family. She edged away, staying near enough for him to find her if he needed her, but far enough away to be out of the fray. She looked at the nearby gravestones, wondering about the other Holts buried there. The family had been in Utah since the late 1800s, and some of the softer stone monuments were weathered to the point that she had difficulty making out names and dates. She examined one of the nearest stones, a gray granite marker with stark, strong lettering.

Jacob Terrence Holt. Beloved son of Terrence and Sophia Holt.

Wait, what? Son? She calculated the birth and death date numbers. He wasn't quite seventeen when he died. She thought back to the eulogy during the funeral. There had been no mention of individual names of family members that had died before Terrence, just a vague reference to those who had gone on before.

Jacob had been Travis's older brother. Clearly, the family didn't speak of him. She recalled the look on Travis's face during their first date when she'd asked about his siblings. The loss of a brother would no doubt have hit him hard, especially when he'd been, what, ten or eleven? She turned this new piece of the puzzle that was Travis over in her mind. What had that loss done to shape him into who he was now?

* * * *

Every night, Travis came to her, quiet, still caught in that numbed yet functional state he'd fallen into after he'd cried for the loss of his father. He had to climb out eventually, but Andri had no idea how to help him. He made love to her urgently, his need so great she could see it in his eyes, filtering through the wall that blocked off the rest of his inner turmoil. He slept poorly, restless in her bed, and as a result, she found herself looking more haggard every morning. Something had to give.

A week after the funeral, Travis sat beside her on his chalet's couch as she worked on the laptop. He'd barely spoken two sentences since she'd arrived an hour earlier, and the silence ate at her. Finally, her patience wearing thin, she closed the laptop and set it on the end table. She turned to Travis, took one of his hands in hers. "Travis. Talk to me."

He glanced at her. "About what?"

She looked him up and down, waving her hand to indicate all of him. "About this. About you."

He sighed, dropping his head against the back of the couch. "I'm not sure what to say."

A chill skittered through her, chased by the thought that he wanted to end their relationship. Surely not. Not with the way he wrapped himself around her every night, seeking comfort. Still. She'd rather ask than be blindsided later. "Do you want to break up, Travis?"

His gaze snapped to hers, more alive than she'd seen him since before the trauma began. "No." His voice was flat but firm.

She chose to take his answer at face value. "Then what's going on inside that head of yours?"

He stood up and paced for a moment. "A lot of things. I feel guilty."

"Why?"

He turned on her. "Why? Seriously? I foisted my brother off on my dad, and now Danny feels like he was that last bit of strain that pushed Dad's heart too far. Plus, if I'd just made Dad go to the doctor, even if I had to force him, he'd still be here."

She frowned. This was heading downhill fast, and though she could see the craziness of his logic from the outside, when she looked at the situation through Travis's lens, he was right. How could she stop this? "You don't know that, Travis."

"Yes, I do." His voice dropped, soft and dripping with pain. "Dad is dead. Mother is devastated. Danny is broken. My aunts and uncles and cousins are hurting. The company employees are all holding their breath, wondering if things will continue on without a major disaster. I know full well I'm on the edge of completely destroying things with you. And it's all. My. Fault. Failure, Andri. It's what I do. It's what I've always done. And I haven't the slightest damned idea how to stop it."

A wave of anger swamped over her, completely unexpected, and snapped her loose from her carefully cultivated moorings. "Travis, what happened to you? I can piece together some of what is going on in your head, but the sheer mass of the responsibility you put on yourself, that I don't get."

"I'm not putting it on myself, Andri. It's mine. It's just the way things are."

She shook her head, tension clawing through every muscle. "I hate to break it to you, *kardia mou*, but you are not the center of the known universe. Everything doesn't fall on your shoulders, but you sure try to stack everything there. And you don't trust anyone else to handle anything, not even their own lives."

Frustration clouded his expression. "You don't understand."

Emotion boiled, raising her volume when she said, "Then make me understand. Explain it to me."

He dropped back onto the couch, leaning back and staring at the ceiling. "I can't."

"At least give me *something* to make it worth putting up with this for the long haul. Do you love me?"

The brilliant flash of panic in his eyes told her she'd pushed as far as she could.

She clamped down on her anger, and on the sudden rush of pain. She bit off a curse and turned away from him. She went out through the sliding glass door onto the deck. Another afternoon thunderstorm gathered over the mountains that made up the spine of the Wasatch. She turned into the wind as it kicked up, drawing deep, calming breaths scented with pine, aspen, and the coming rain.

He didn't follow her outside, and honestly, she hadn't expected him to. She was losing him. Not to another woman, or a hobby, or work, or even fading interest. She was losing him to the dark vortex that swirled around him, sucking at his soul, keeping him mired in the misery of his misplaced guilt.

Andri separated herself from the emotions breaking over her, then processed the situation, calculating her options. There were only so many choices. Stay and do nothing, hoping he eventually pulled himself free of his baggage. Stay and nag him to change, and she knew better than to think that might actually work.

Suddenly, the pieces clicked into place and she knew what she had to do. Once it dawned on her, she realized it was really the only choice. The only thing she could do that might help push Travis to find his way out of his prison. Her heart ripped in two the moment she accepted it, and the pain sucked the air from her lungs. She waited for a few seconds until she had enough self-control to proceed. It had to be now. Before she found a way to stop herself.

She walked back into the chalet, coming to a stop a few feet in front of where he still sat on the couch.

"Travis. You're letting yourself stay anchored in a dark place in your world. You're not ready to move forward. If I stick around, you're never going to be ready, and I'll keep making excuses for you and trying to help you without really being any help at all. I can't allow myself to do that. For both our sakes."

She watched as panic infused his gaze. "Andri, what are you doing?" He rose, crossed the distance between them. He reached for her, but she shook her head, taking a step back.

Panic crossed into desperation. "Andri, please."

Completely calm now, she stepped forward and put a hand on his chest, the other bracketing his face. "Listen to me, because I want you to remember this. I love you, Travis. I will always love you. But you need to get yourself in a better place. You need to learn to let go and not assume responsibility for your entire sphere of existence. Heal yourself, *kardia mou.* When and if you do, come to me."

She rose on her toes and pressed her lips to his. He might have been granite for all he responded. She picked up her laptop and purse and left, never turning back.

There was one thing of which she was completely certain. When the calm wore off, she was going to second-guess every word she had just spoken.

The calm carried her into the car. Tears began rolling down her cheeks before she got her seatbelt on.

Her strength gave out halfway to Park City. She pulled off the next freeway exit, onto the shoulder at the bottom of the hill, and turned off the car just as the first wave of sobs sliced through her, cutting her to ribbons. The anguish bent her forward, crushing her under the intense pressure.

Andri cried until her throat grew raw, until her muscles ached from being clenched, until her stomach threatened to empty itself under the brute force of her pain. The storm finally subsided, leaving her drained, body and soul.

She waited until her breath smoothed out, until she regained enough composure to be safe on the road. Then she pulled her car around and headed for Rachel's house, avoiding thoughts of Travis and how much he might be hurting right now.

* * * *

Travis's feet unfroze moments after Andri walked out of his home. He raced out onto the front steps in time to see her swipe a hand across her cheek, wiping away tears, then drive away. Dazed, he went back inside. He kicked the door shut, cursing, and slammed his fists against the wall.

And then the onslaught hit, driving him to his knees. His heart shattered, the intense sorrow ripping his soul, searing him from the inside out, until he felt like ash on the wind.

He knew it. He knew it would end badly, damn it, and he pursued her anyway. She tilted his world on its axis and pulled him free from the morass so he could breathe. She was everything he wanted, everything he needed her to be, but what he knew from the beginning held true. She, with her warm heart and kryptonite smile, was the last thing tossed on the pile, the rock that pushed him under.

She'd said she loved him, and, God, that was the worst part. She'd given him everything, body, soul, heart, mind. He'd betrayed her in his own way, unable to show her all of his failures, unable to tell her how much she meant to him. He'd broken her heart, after he'd sworn never to do to another person what Melody had done to him. But he had done it to Andri. She'd given him her whole heart. He'd held his back, and kept his darkest secrets. He'd unbalanced their relationship, and it had crashed.

Travis stripped off his clothes and tossed himself onto his bed, staring at the ceiling, seething inside. What in the hell was wrong with him, that he couldn't just let go and love her? Nothing about her resembled his mother, or Melody, or any other woman, for that matter. She came to him with an open heart, offering him the world on a string, and he couldn't reach out and take it.

Three little words he'd not said to a woman in a long, long time. Three little words that had torn holes in his soul every time he'd used them. He tried to say them, and his throat constricted, his heart pounded behind its cage.

It broke him to know he had failed her, like he failed everyone else. Now it was over. She'd learn to hate him. It wasn't that far from loving him, after all. She'd find her way there.

Why couldn't he say it? He wanted to say it, to tell her he loved her more than anything, that he needed her more than he needed air. He wanted her here, wanted to spend the rest of his life with her.

He didn't know how to break free. And it had just cost him everything.

Chapter Fourteen

Andri pulled into Rachel's driveway on her way home from Travis's place. Rachel answered the door, her expression darkening as she took in Andri's appearance, and ushered her in to sit at the kitchen table. Rachel grabbed two spoons and a carton of moose tracks ice cream then dropped into the chair beside her.

She handed Andri a spoon. "What the hell happened? You look awful."

Andri smiled weakly. "Thanks so much."

The ice cream really didn't appeal to her until she'd swallowed a spoonful. Once she started eating and talking, the words gushed out of her. She told Rachel everything that had gone on and how she'd responded. "I feel terrible, Rach. You know how I feel about channeling my mother, but I couldn't help it. The whole situation made me so angry!"

Rachel swallowed and shook her head. "Andri, I have never, ever heard you yell at someone, unless they were ten rows down at the football stadium and you were trying to get their attention."

Andri thought about that for a moment. As much as she didn't want to turn into her father, she even more vehemently did not wish to turn into her mother. She'd worked hard to excise the urge to scream while arguing from her system, but that urge had surfaced with a vengeance with Travis. She sighed. "I did raise my voice. I managed to not scream at him, though."

"Well, a raised voice he had coming. Probably had screaming coming too, but I know how much that bothers you, so I'm glad you held it back."

"Thanks."

Rachel's brow furrowed. "Did you come straight here from the showdown?"

Andri shook her head. "No. Pulled off the road for a world-class collapse and cry."

Rachel's expression grew sorrowful. "I thought so. You look like you fell apart."

"I did. I'm just kind of numb inside now." Andri sat back in her chair, setting her spoon on the table. "Did I do the wrong thing?"

Rachel considered the remainder of the ice cream. Andri could practically see the wheels turning in her head. "You know, I think there wasn't much else you could do." She looked at Andri for a while, then sighed. "He wasn't always this bad. I mean, yeah, carrying the weight of the free world on his shoulders? He's done that as far back as I can remember. But everything that happened in his life added something to his burdens that he never let go. Danny's issues hurt him. Melody hurt him and sort of shut him down, but I don't think she did much more to him than any other painful event in his life."

"What happened? What did she do?" She needed to know, though gathering yet another piece of the puzzle that was Travis made her heart start to ache a little again.

"To be honest, I don't know. No one does. Travis refused to talk about it. I asked him once, and he just said, 'She left.' Knowing him, though, knowing how he throws his heart and soul into everything he does, that's really all she had to do, especially with all the other shit he keeps bottled up inside. The fact that she walked away, on top of a pile of things he's never let go, was enough to push him under."

Andri nodded slowly. That made sense. Especially if the correlation she'd put together before, between his mother and his ex, held true. "I love him, you know."

Rachel reached over and ruffled her hair. "I know."

"I believe that he wants to be with me."

"I'd be shocked if he didn't."

Andri couldn't shake the feeling that Rachel was hedging, holding back on something in this discussion. "I'd give anything to get to the bottom of Travis's mind and understand why he puts so much on himself. There's a genesis to all of this, I know there is."

Rachel looked away and shrugged. "It's the mystery of the ages."

Andri's eyes narrowed, reading her friend's body language. "You know more than you want to tell me."

Rachel left the table, silence in her wake. She tossed the empty carton in the garbage under the sink and placed their spoons in the dishwasher. Andri followed her out onto the back deck and stood beside her friend at the railing, looking out over the dark yard, moonlight sparkling on the leaves and grass still wet from the storm that had blown through earlier.

Rachel sighed and rubbed her eyes. "Andri. Has he ever told you about Jacob?"

Her mind flashed back to the marker near Terrence's plot. The unmentioned son. "His older brother, right?" At Rachel's nod, she said, "I read his headstone at the cemetery. He died young."

"Yes, he did. When the time comes that you talk to Travis again, ask him about Jacob. And tell him I love him and it's for his own good that I mentioned it."

A shiver ran down Andri's spine, and at that moment, she wasn't altogether certain she wanted to know the story of Jacob after all.

* * * *

Travis stared at his phone for the hundredth time. That was an improvement. The first day without Andri, he'd stared at it for hours at a time, willing her to call, to text. The next few days after that, he'd stared trying to convince himself to call or text her. But she didn't want to talk to him right now, and he'd respect her wishes, even if it drained out every drop of color and light and warmth in his life.

He climbed out of his truck and grabbed his tool belt. It was hotter than hell today, but he couldn't stomach being in the office. The framing crew made room for him, accepting him on the team to get walls built and lifted on this custom home.

Andri was right, he thought as he worked. He was broken. He'd known it for a long time, deep down, but he'd used all his strength to run from the truth, as if by ignoring it and acting as if he was fine, and making everyone around him fine, that his own truth would change.

It hadn't.

The biggest problem with being broken, aside from leaving him with nothing to give Andri, was that he couldn't go back to what he'd been. He couldn't be the Travis who stuffed everything away and pretended it was all okay. He had one option at this point. He could face himself and try to find a way to build something new.

He was at the bottom of a deep, dark pit, but fortunately, that bottom was bedrock. No way for him to dig deeper. This was as far as he could drop. Funny. He'd always imagined he'd shatter completely if he fell this far. Yes, he was in pieces, but he wasn't disintegrating. There were actual pieces to rebuild and shape into something better. That gave him hope.

And Andri? His muscles strained as he and two other guys lifted a wall into place. That whisper from the darkest part of him still lived, and it said Andri'd never want him again. Not broken, not repaired. But he examined the delicate image of her in his mind. The smile that never failed to send a bolt of sunshine through his heart. Her intelligence, patience, wisdom.

She understood him better than anyone had. Only now did he realize that when someone knew you that well, they could show you truths about yourself that you didn't like. She didn't do it to be cruel, but because that's what someone who loved you was supposed to do. Help you see your own reality and make it better. Or appreciate what you had in the first place.

And she did love him. It startled him to realize that he didn't question her declaration in any way. It was a fact. Simple, pure. She loved him, even when she saw his weaknesses. Of course, she didn't know the worst of his failures yet. But where he lacked faith in himself, he realized he did have faith in her. In her love for him.

Pedro, one of his head framers, stopped on his way to the open doorway. He looked worried, but smiled, his teeth white against his dark-tanned skin and black mustache. "Hey, boss. Lunch time. Lupe sent me with tamales today, but no way I'm gonna eat so many. Why don't you come help me out, huh?"

Travis paused for a moment, then laid the nail gun on the plywood floor and gave Pedro a half-smile. "Sounds good." He hadn't eaten well in days, but if he was going to do the work to get his head on straight, he'd need some food in his system.

And he definitely had work to do before he returned to Andri. All he could do was pray she was still there when that time came.

* * * *

Travis noticed Danny in the office every day, starting a week after the funeral. With his workload, he spoke to his brother only in brief sentences, always about work, and rarely in person. Something had to change. One evening, after everyone else had gone and the sound of some alternative band with a fierce beat thumped on the airwaves from his brother's office, Travis walked in to see him.

Dan looked up from his desk where he sat reading a letter, then pressed the button to turn off the speakers. "What's up?"

His brother had changed, and Travis was ashamed to realize he didn't know when it had happened. Danny had cut his long hair just shy of military short, making the angles of his face that much more defined. He'd added another thick, solid slash and sharp curves to the heavy black tattoo on his left arm, newly visible below his t-shirt sleeve. Enduring that much ink had to hurt like hell. Travis shoved his hands in his jeans pockets. "How's it going?"

Danny's brow furrowed. "On which job?"

"No, not work-wise. How are things with you?"

He shrugged, his well-worn defiant expression appearing. "Good. Clean. Mostly sober. Nothing for you to worry about."

The bite in Danny's voice hurt. He remembered that moment when Andri asked him if he ever really spent time with his brother on a personal level. Shame burned in his gut when he faced the truth head-on. No. He didn't. It had become all about battling the addiction.

He'd kept the pamphlets and other handouts he'd found on his father's desk. Last night, he'd taken the time to read them, with an open mind, trying to learn. His brother had a long way to go to heal. So did he. This was only the first of many changes he needed to make.

"Danny." He pulled up a chair and dropped into it, putting himself level with his brother. "Can we just talk for a bit? For real?"

Danny eyed him with suspicion. "Why?"

"Because I've been so busy trying to act like a keeper that I've forgotten how to be a brother. And I'd really like to know how you're doing."

Danny sat back. He stared at his desk for a moment, myriad emotions flashing across his sharp features. Travis forced himself to wait patiently while his brother worked through things in his own head. Finally, he looked up and gave Travis the first genuine smile, tentative but real, that he'd seen from Danny in a very long time.

"I'm getting there, Trav. But, I…this time I'm approaching it for real. I'm trying to get the depression handled. I've started on a new prescription."

Wow. In the world of Danny, admitting he needed help and then actually taking that help, especially antidepressants, was huge. "That's great."

"Yeah. I have a good doc. He told me to hang in there, and if this one doesn't work, there are other options. He promised we'll figure it out if I'm willing to work with him. And I have my twelve-step sponsor, and the counselor he referred me to. I think I can do this, you know? And I have to. I, um…"

His voice wavered, then died. He scrubbed a hand across his short hair in a motion very familiar to Travis. "I promised Dad. When he drove me home that night. He drove two hours to pick me up when all I wanted was money to keep playing. And, of all things, he said he was proud of me for not falling too far that time. Can you believe that? Just because I wasn't totally blitzed when I called him. Made me feel like shit."

The sheer loathing in Danny's voice made Travis's heart ache. "I can only imagine."

Danny drew a shuddering breath. "I wanted to make him proud for real. So, in the hospital, I promised him." His eyes were red when he lifted his gaze to meet Travis's. "Can I ask you a question, Trav?"

He swallowed hard, unsure if his voice would work through the lump in his throat. "Yeah?"

Danny fell silent for a moment, then finally said, "It feels like my fault that Dad's dead. Maybe, if I hadn't called that night, if he hadn't made that drive. I mean, I shouldn't have put that stress on him."

Compassion pressed hard on Travis's chest. "Dan, don't. It's not your fault. But I understand. I feel like it's my fault too."

Danny's brow creased in confusion. "Why?"

No way in hell would he say *because I told you to call him*, though he did feel terrible guilt about that. It wouldn't make Danny feel better in any way, so he kept it to himself. "Because I knew he wasn't feeling well, and I tried to get him in for a checkup. I should have tried harder, or taken him myself."

Danny cocked his head to the side, looking at him. "Travis, just because you're the oldest son doesn't mean everything is your responsibility. If Dad knew he wasn't well, he should have gone to the doctor. That's his error, not yours, not by a long shot. And Mother had to know he wasn't doing so hot, She could have said something. Hell, maybe she did. Dad was stubborn. He probably didn't listen to her either."

Travis thought about that for a while. "It still feels like my fault."

"Still feels like mine."

After a moment of silence, Travis gave voice to something his office manager had suggested to him the other day, when she'd noticed him struggling. "Maybe it's not anyone's fault. Maybe it's just one of those awful damn things that happens."

Somehow it felt too easy to call it *one of those things*.

Danny considered the idea for a moment. "Nobody's fault? I've used that to excuse a lot of things when it wasn't true."

"Yeah, I know. But maybe this time it is the truth. It's kind of a strange concept for me, but I think I might try it on for size. See how it feels."

Danny nodded. "I think you should. Probably be good for you."

Travis smiled, surprised at how good a little brotherly absolution made him feel. Then he sobered. "Danny, can you forgive me for not really being there as a brother?"

Danny blew out a breath, shaking his head. "Trav, you've always been there. Maybe not always the way I wanted you to be, but you've been there anyway. Besides, I understand why you are the way you are."

Travis frowned. "What are you talking about?"

"You try to save me because of Jacob."

His gut churned, darkness and sludge filling him. "I worry about you for your own sake, Dan."

"I believe that. But, I've watched you try to wrangle with the memory of Jacob all these years. I know you thought no one noticed. I did, though."

Travis sat in stunned silence. He'd tried so hard to keep that first, greatest failing shoved down in the darkest recesses of his soul. How the hell had Danny seen it? How could he have known what he struggled with, when Danny was little more than a toddler when it happened? "It's a lot to wrangle with."

"Doesn't need to be. That wasn't your fault, any more than Dad, or my ration of shit was your fault or responsibility."

"You and I obviously remember things differently."

"Then you need to think about it with a clearer vision."

"Danny, you were five."

Danny laughed without humor in it. "And you were ten. You were ten, and he was sixteen. Think about that, Trav." Danny leaned toward him over the desk. "Seriously. Put it in perspective. You were ten, just like cousin Holly's twins. A scrawny ten-year-old versus a kid twice your size, a teenager with a death wish. What exactly do you think you could have done to stop him? How can you imagine it could've gone differently?"

The shock sent a cold sweat breaking over his skin. Danny broke down the most awful part of his life from a polar opposite point of view and it left him speechless. His thoughts churned. Yes, he'd only been ten, but he remembered everything with such clarity...didn't he? Had he ever put his age in context?

"I never really thought of it like that." Holly's kids were cute, precocious, and entertaining to listen to for a while between their moments of annoying, but they were children. The difference between them and his cousin Sean, who'd turned sixteen in January—damn, they were a world apart. In his memories, he and Jacob were on the same level, but how could they have been, really?

He'd become the eldest son after Jacob died, and Dad had impressed on him the understanding of responsibility that came with being the oldest. Had that all run together until it became exaggerated and twisted inside him?

It left him unsettled, with a great deal to think about. He was starting to see that much of the torture he'd suffered over the years might have been self-inflicted. And here he thought Danny was the one with all the issues. His brother's were just more obvious than his own.

He shook himself free from thoughts he knew he'd have to go back to before he could completely let them go. "Dan, do you want to go do something sometime?"

His brother grinned, but gave Travis a non-committal shrug. "Dunno. Are you any fun to hang out with?"

"I have my moments. Do you still waterski?" It shamed him to realize he didn't know what Danny enjoyed anymore.

"No. I like to hike though."

Travis stood and stretched. "I haven't bagged a peak in a while. Want to go climb a mountain next week?"

Danny's eyes lit up. "Pfeifferhorn? That should kick both our asses."

He stifled a groan. That was a bit more mountain than he had in mind, but it could've been worse. At least Danny didn't suggest Lone Peak. "You're on."

* * * *

Travis found his mother one Friday morning, standing in front of her wild flower garden, gloves and floppy sunhat in one hand. Travis had checked on her every day in the weeks since the funeral. She wasn't coping terribly well, but then, who among them was? He waited for a moment, watching her as she stared at the beds, as if she wasn't really seeing them. He didn't think she'd seen him, either, until she spoke.

"This garden always amused him, your father."

She never spoke to him about anything to do with her relationship with Dad. He barely breathed, afraid to say anything that might stop her from talking.

"He said that people looking at my garden were seeing the real me and they didn't know it. It was his greatest secret on display, and no one ever realized."

He looked from his mother to the overgrown garden and back again. How could that possibly be her, his mother who never let a hair out of place, who defined refinement and elegance, who insisted on perfection in every last detail?

She carefully settled the sunhat over her hair. "Even he didn't realize how right he was. It's unruly now, neglected rather than free. I haven't worked out here in a very long time. I paid someone to weed it on occasion, but even that fell by the wayside. I haven't bothered to add anything new. And I finally understand why."

His heart pounded when she turned to face him. "Why, Mother?"

"Because this is where I put my heartache. I came out here to plant a bleeding heart a week after we lost Jacob. I thought I could leave the suffering here with the flower. Instead I ended up leaving my joy, too.

"I left that part of myself here, instead of giving it to you and to Daniel. I'm sorry, Travis. I let you down."

The bruised child hidden deep inside of him peeked out, seeking warmth from her apology. The adult in him cringed to hear her cut herself like that, but when he shook his head and opened his mouth to absolve her, she said, "No, Travis. Don't tell me what I want to hear. The truth is what it is. Let me own it."

She was still his cool, pleasant, but impassive mother. If she didn't want to let him placate her self-doubt, perhaps there was one thing she would accept from him. Something he hadn't said to her in a very long time. "I love you."

Tears shimmered in her eyes for a moment before she swallowed them back. "Thank you. I love you, too."

The awkwardness stretched but snapped off abruptly when she looked down at her hands and pulled on the gardening gloves. "Well, then," she said briskly. "I have a great deal to do if I'm going to reclaim this garden. I'd better get started."

She turned away, sank to her knees, and began to pull out weeds. Only now, he saw it for what it was—repairing and reclaiming herself.

* * * *

He hadn't seen Andri in weeks, and though he'd had plenty of work to do, on far more than his job, he couldn't bear the loss of her any longer. It was time to secure the most important relationship in his life.

He drove to her apartment Friday night. He'd waited long enough to catch her at home even if she'd put in one of her twelve hour days. Her car was in its space. Good. His heart pounded in anticipation as he walked up to her door. He knocked.

No response. Maybe she was in the shower. That thought kicked up a flare of heat deep inside that he tamped down. Later. He slipped his key in the lock and let himself in.

One light was on in the kitchen, but the silence in the apartment struck him. Was she asleep? It wasn't that late. Fluffball jumped up on a nearby chair and meowed for attention.

"Hey, buddy." He scratched the cat's back. "Where's my girl?"

He checked her bedroom, the bathroom, tension growing by the moment. He looked into her office. No laptop. A few pages sat on the printer tray. The internet address printed on the bottom of the pages looked like it might have been an email she printed, taking what she needed on the first page and leaving behind the excess ads and junk. Ads for rental cars, hotels...where was she going?

He gave Fluffball some attention before he left. He called Andri on the way to his truck. No answer. Was she avoiding him?

There was only one place he could think of to go now. He drove, not wanting to call for fear of what he might hear over the phone. He cursed the length of the drive, but his luck wasn't all bad tonight. The lights were on at Rachel's when he finally reached her house. She opened the door, she gave him a once-over and stepped back to let him in. "She's not here."

"What, I can't come see my oldest friend just because I miss her company?"

Rachel shook her head. "Oh, please. Though I think you probably owe me dinner. Or a movie. That would be nice."

She went to the kitchen, and he followed, settling on a chair at the table while she reached into the refrigerator for drinks. "Rach, it pains me to see you sitting home alone."

She met him at the table and handed him a bottle of beer. "I don't mind. Beats the dating meat market."

"You're amazing, you know. You'll find someone."

Her gaze flickered, exposing a cloud of confusion for just a moment before it cleared. "It's just a matter of time." Then she waved a hand at him, moving on. "But, you're not here about my lack of a love life, you're here about your own."

He stared at her for a moment, realizing in a flash how much more he'd gotten from their friendship than he'd given over the years. "I'm sorry, Rachel."

"For what?"

"Being such a selfish friend."

"Travis." She leaned across the table and squeezed his hand. "You've always been there when I've needed you. We're cool."

"You sure?"

"Yep. Cool enough to tell you that Andri is out of town."

"I thought she might be. On business?"

"Nah. She had the day off today, some company thing, so she flew to New York last night to see her brother for the weekend."

Fear rattled his insides. What were the chances that she'd decide to stay there? "Everything okay?"

"She needed a little change of scenery."

He nodded, staring at the table. Damn. He really didn't want to wait until she came back. He needed to see her now. He'd worked through so much of the crap he'd hauled around inside of him. Now, it was down to her. To them.

He had two choices. Stay where he was, apprehensive, worried about the possibility of another relationship crumbling in his hands. Or move forward. Go for broke and possibly end up miserable, or not move and be ripped to pieces anyway.

It had to be forward.

He stood, then leaned down and grabbed Rachel in a tight hug. When he kissed her on the cheek and released her, she looked stunned.

"What was that for?"

"For you being you. For being my friend. For putting up with all of my bullshit over the years."

"Um. Okay. Not sure who you are or what you've done with Travis, but okay. You're welcome."

Travis started toward the door. She called after him, "Where are you going?"

He pulled the door open and tossed a grin at her over his shoulder. "Where else? New York."

Chapter Fifteen

Andri went into the kitchen and washed her hands at the sink, looking out over the expanse of lawn and trees that made up her brother's back yard. This was the first time she'd visited since he bought the gorgeous colonial in Hyde Park last year, and a part of her never wanted to leave. She loved the hardwood floors and the ten-foot ceilings and the acre yard just begged for someone to garden. The fact that it was practically walking distance to the Hudson was a major plus.

"Andri?" Dmitri's deep voice carried through the house from the entry.

"I'm in the kitchen." The house was far too big for her bachelor brother, but she knew he intended to spend his life here, so he'd planned ahead for the needs of an eventual family. He was a man who deserved to be happily married, raising a couple of kids, enjoying weekends running the boat on the river.

They'd been out on the boat all afternoon, she and Dmitri and a couple of his friends. The trees on the hills overlooking the Hudson had just started changing color for autumn, and the beauty did her soul some good. She'd make another trip in a few weeks, maybe, to see everything in full color. For now, she needed to clean up before her brother took her to dinner.

She heard him enter the kitchen behind her and she turned. "So what's the proper dress for this restaurant?"

Anything else she might have said fled at the sight of Travis standing behind Dmitri. Heart pounding, she focused on her brother. He wore his lawyer face, completely impervious to interpretation.

"Andri, you have company. I'll be upstairs if you need anything." Dmitri turned, nodded once to Travis, then left the room.

She shifted to look at Travis, her pulse thumping hard and loud in her ears. He wore gray jeans, a white t-shirt under an open red flannel shirt, and a bit of scruffy stubble shadowed his jaw. He looked yummy without even trying, and she clamped down on her cell-deep response, crossing her arms in a desperate need to protect herself from his draw on her heart. The magnetic pull made her lean back against the counter to balance herself, to keep herself from falling into his arms. It had only been a few weeks since she'd seen him, but oh, God, she'd missed him like she'd miss water, or sunlight, or warmth, if similarly deprived. But the situation was delicate and she had to keep her brain firmly in charge here. "Hey."

"Hey. You look great."

"I'm all windblown. Smell like the river, too."

"I like a girl who smells like the river sometimes."

Damn, he always made her stomach flip. "What are you doing here, Travis?"

"I heard you'd gone to see your brother. I figured I'd come out and meet him." He didn't move toward her, instead choosing to tuck his hands in the pockets of his jeans and lean against the door jamb.

"What did you think of him?"

"Nice guy. I like him." Now he did move, taking a single step toward her, ratcheting her pulse up another notch. "He did give me a bit of grief outside, but I had it coming."

"Oh really? And what did he say?"

Another step closer. "I introduced myself and he said, 'oh, you're the reason my baby sister is upset.' And that hurt. I never want to be the person who upsets you."

She appreciated this little reminder that the brother who had picked on her in their youth still refused to let anyone else in the world give her grief. She loved Dmitri more than ever in that moment. "You're a guy, I'm a girl, *upset* is going to happen sometimes. Comes with the territory."

"True. But I'd rather it be little, momentary upsets. Because I forgot to take the garbage out or I missed the tenth anniversary of our third date or something."

Another step placed him directly in front of her, and her pulse soared, her breath coming faster. She licked her dry lips and his focus zeroed in on her mouth.

"We've had some much bigger upsets," Travis said, his voice softening. "And those I don't ever want to repeat."

"Neither do I." If he touched her, she feared she'd collapse into his arms like some silly little girl. The very air around them crackled with the feeling of something momentous, and she needed her brain fully engaged before her heart agreed to something foolish. "Did my brother say anything else before he unleashed you on me?"

He shrugged. "Maybe. A few things. Standard big brother language, requirements, conditions, that sort of thing."

Her eyebrows arched. "Conditions?"

"Well. One condition. But I'm getting ahead of myself. There's a lot to catch you up on since you smacked me in the head with the verbal two by four."

She winced. Yeah, that was accurate. "I'm sorry."

He chuckled. "If I recall correctly what you said once before, no you're not. Not for what you said, anyway, because it needed saying. It really did. You're incredibly adept at telling me what I don't want to hear."

"Then I'm sorry for the timing. It was a lot to hit you with at that moment. I'm ashamed to admit that I do have some of my mom's temper."

"If that's as pissed off as you ever get, I'll consider myself a lucky man."

His expression grew serious, his eyes turbulent but without a hint of the wall she'd grown accustomed to seeing inside him. "How are things, Travis?"

"Improving. I had a legitimate, heartfelt conversation with my mother. Well, as much of one as I could ever hope to have. It was good. I did the same with my brother. That was even better. He and I are hanging out."

Relief swamped her. "Oh, really?"

"Yeah. Climbing another mountain next week. It'll be fun, if it doesn't kill me. The last one nearly did." He stepped back, giving her a moment to breathe. "Now, there's something important I want to tell you about. It's kind of a long story, so maybe we could sit down somewhere?"

Her insides twisted in response. So far he'd offered good news, but this sounded more serious. Now that she'd seen him and realized just how deeply she'd missed him, she wasn't sure she could take something bad. Her lingering sense of inadequacy surfaced, anticipating the worst. Luckily, her good sense beat back the pathetic, whiny voice shouting scary *what ifs* and reminded her that he wouldn't bother to come all the way to New York to permanently break up with her. She needed to rise to the occasion and listen to his story.

She waggled her fingers at him to follow and she led him into the formal room near the front of the house where Dmitri housed his baby grand piano. She sat on one of the damask love seats and patted the burgundy cushion beside her.

Travis joined her, but, thankfully, he didn't reach out for her. Their knees touched, and that warm connection reminded her just how deeply she'd missed him, but didn't distract her entirely.

He blew out a breath. "Did Rachel ever mention Jacob?"

"In a very cryptic way, yes. After our last, um, upset. We were talking about the pieces of your puzzle."

"That's an interesting way to put it."

"And accurate. Anyway, I'd noticed his name at the cemetery. She suggested I ask you about him. She said to tell that you she loves you and it's for your own good that she mentioned it." Her stomach flipped, and not in a good way. Nerves kicked up, making her hands tremble until she folded them together in her lap.

Travis gave her a half-smile. "I do love that woman. She has a knack for doling out just the right bit of information when it's needed."

"She does."

He held her gaze, his own turbulent. "Jacob was my older brother. He killed himself when I was ten."

Oh, damn, that was a sharp left turn she wasn't expecting. It sucked the breath from her lungs. As she reminded herself to breathe, she realized that, for once, Travis wasn't hiding a thing in his expression. He let her see the pain. Pain that touched her soul-deep, made her ache with the desire to soothe him. "Travis, I can't even imagine how that hurt."

"It did. It damaged us all. But here's the thing. I was convinced it was my fault."

"How could it possibly have been your fault?"

"I found him in the bathroom, talking to himself in the mirror. He was holding a gun he'd stolen from a friend's dad."

Sickness roiled inside her, leaving her unsure she wanted to know the truth, but determined to listen if he was going to talk about it. "What happened?"

"I knew something bad was going to happen. I could feel it in the air. So I tried to take the gun away from him. I fought for that gun until he punched me in the stomach and shoved me out of the bathroom. He locked the door." His voice grew rough and the darkness in his eyes pierced her heart. "When I got my wind back, I pounded and kicked the door, but he wouldn't answer me. It finally occurred to me to call my mom and dad. They'd gone to dinner. Jacob was babysitting us."

Andri reached for his hand, clutching him with trembling fingers. Understanding tore a hole in her soul and left tears streaming down her cheeks. "By the time they got home…"

He nodded. "Too late. Every time something goes wrong now, especially with Danny, I fight with Jacob in my dreams. I hear that gunshot over and over."

She wiped her cheeks and folded her fingers over his. "You felt like you should have stopped him."

"Yes. It took Danny to help me finally put it in perspective, but I've always felt responsible. After his death, my mother pulled away from us. Which meant I was responsible for that, too."

The rest of the pieces rapidly clicked into place. Oh, he made so much more sense now. "And then Danny and his problems."

"It just kept building. I felt responsible for it all, and I failed people who were everything to me. Then came Melody."

Andri ached for what he'd gone through, for what he'd done to himself all those years, all that needless suffering. She tightened her grip on his hand. "I do have a bit of a theory about Melody."

He squeezed her hand in return. "Oh, really? What's that?"

She felt the strength in his grip and realized how steady, how open he was now. His healing was well underway, and her heart lifted. "My theory is that you married a woman a lot like your mom. To try to fix what you couldn't."

"Not bad, detective. I've thought about that a lot lately. I tried to make Melody happy because I loved her, and so I wouldn't fail at being married. About the only close personal relationship I haven't screwed up is with Rachel, though we've had our moments over the years. Even with my dad, look where we ended up."

Andri reached out, laying a hand against his cheek. "You can't blame yourself for that."

"I know. But that's where my brain naturally wants to go with it. Anyway, I digress. Melody's similarity to my mother stopped at withholding emotional intimacy, and for very different reasons. Melody liked having all the control, and she wielded intimacy in all its forms like a weapon to get what she wanted. But the fact that she was never satisfied was far bigger than our marriage. When she decided the grass was greener elsewhere, she left."

He blew out a deep breath, his expression lighter, as if he had finally released everything that tortured him. "So. That's it. My litany of failure. I've realized that I held onto those failures. In my own way, they were my shield from being hurt by anything new. They were my protective armor."

Travis took both her hands in his and her pulse skittered. Oh, God, she'd missed him so much. "But there was no way to protect myself from you. That first day you smiled at me, you have no idea. You ripped right through me. You opened me up all the way to the core, and what blew my mind was that you accepted me. And you scared me so much that I pushed back.

"I'll be honest with you, sweetheart. You still scare the hell out of me. But I have to trust what you show me is real, because I've never seen anything in you that isn't real. Even now, you're sitting there looking at me with such calmness. How do you do that?"

She smiled at him, her heart soaring at his closeness, his openness. She'd dared to hope that he'd find his way out of his morass, that he'd come back to her. To have him here, now, filled her soul to bursting with joy. "I'm calm because I'm completely aware of what I have and what I want. What was my brother's condition that you mentioned earlier?"

"He said he'd only let me in if I was absolutely certain how I feel."

Her heart skipped. "And are you?"

"One hundred percent."

He left the love seat and took a knee in front of her. Time slowed and her heartbeat pulsed frantically in her ears. His deep blue gaze held her in place. *Oh, God, yes, please.*

"Andri." His hands trembled slightly around hers. "I want you in my life. I want to fall asleep with you in my arms and wake up with you the next morning, forever. I need you more than I can explain. I love you."

He released one hand and reached into his pocket. He took her hand again, placing something warm and hard in her palm. "Andromeda," he said, his voice ragged. "Please. Be my wife."

In her hand lay a gorgeous ring of platinum leaves, woven around a stunning square diamond, smaller diamonds nestled between the leaves. She closed her fingers over the shining symbol and screamed, "Yes!"

Andri threw herself into Travis's arms, and he caught her, laughing. "I do love your enthusiasm."

"Yes, yes, yes," she said, her voice growing softer, until she breathed *yes* against his mouth. Then his lips captured hers, a hungry groan issuing from his throat as he kissed her. She fiercely returned his kiss, her tongue seeking his. Her entire frame shuddered with need.

In the one remaining part of her brain that still functioned, it occurred to Andri that Dmitri should have made an appearance by now. Shei pulled back far enough to capture Travis's gaze. "Did you tell Dmitri what you were planning to do? Because he didn't come running when I screamed like a crazy woman."

"Nope. I just showed him the ring."

"Cool." And then the ability to think in simple words was lost in the heat of his kiss.

She had gone to Utah seeking a safe haven. He had come into her life needing asylum, too, and together, they had found the refuge they both desperately needed. As Andri pulled her husband-to-be to his feet, she knew they would shelter each other forever.

Epilogue

"What are you saying?" Andri's mom, Zoe Miller, shrieked in his mother's kitchen, where she, Andri, and Sophia were supposed to be chatting and making dinner. "You've never made him baklava? How is that possible?"

Travis laughed at the dismay and outrage in Zoe's voice. He sat on the recliner in the great room, putting the foot rest up as Zoe strode in, hands gesturing dramatically as she carried on in Greek. She was a tiny thing, an inch or so shorter than Andri, her hair impossibly black for her age. This was the second time she'd left Phoenix and come for a visit since he'd asked Andri to marry him last September, and while she could be very entertaining, he didn't mind driving her back to the airport when the time came as well. Andri was right. Her mom was a bit of a diva.

Andri came into the room, twisting her long, gorgeous hair into a ponytail. "Ma, really, it isn't my best dish. He likes my spanakopita, and I make tzatziki all the time." His stomach rumbled at the mention of food. If dinner was dependent on Zoe staying focused in the kitchen, it might be a while before he ate.

Zoe ranted and gesticulated at Andri until his fiancée was pinching the bridge of her nose in an obvious bid for patience.

Suddenly, her mom turned and marched over to stand at his side, looking down at him. She put on a lovely smile. "Travis, I apologize for my daughter." Her tone had shifted into perfect sweetness and light, and he reconsidered Andri's description. Zoe was a *lot* of a diva.

His future mother-in-law grasped his hand with one of hers, patting his forearm with the other. "I can assure you she makes an excellent baklava. It's something every Greek woman should know, and she promises to prove that she does and make it for tomorrow's dessert."

"Thank you, Zoe." He smiled, giving her hand a squeeze, turning up his own charm. He'd had to work a bit to win her over the first time they met, but he knew how to talk to her now. "What I most want right now is to dig into your cooking. Whatever you're making smells fantastic."

She blushed, a dusting of pink that reminded him of Andri, the first time they met. Zoe patted his arm again. "Such a charmer. Let me go check the lamb. It should be ready soon."

As she left, Travis shifted his gaze back to Andri, who leaned against the wall, pulling her pink cardigan close around her. Warmth and happiness glowed in her expressive brown eyes when she smiled at him. It didn't matter that she wore an old pair of jeans, didn't have any makeup on, beat him in every video game except the racing ones, and had made him agree to watch her favorite British TV shows and learn to fly fish before she would set a wedding date. She was perfect. Even her flaws were perfect. Well, perfect for him. That's all that mattered.

He opened his arms to her. "Come here, sweetheart."

Andri joined him, and he grabbed her hips. She shrieked as he pulled her onto his lap, then giggled. Travis nuzzled her neck, breathing in her scent. He drew his tongue along the shell of her ear and she whimpered softly. Her breath hitched when he shifted under her, ensuring she felt what she'd done to him, without even trying.

While Zoe was in town, she stayed with Andri. Which left him sleeping in his own home, in his own bed, very much alone. They'd both snuck out from work for a couple of lunch quickies, but he was tiring of sleeping by himself.

He set his teeth against her earlobe, making her breath catch again. "I miss you, Andromeda."

She adjusted her position, sliding her hips over him, and he stifled a groan. "Miss you too, *kardia mou*. So, so, so much."

A snicker and the gentle clearing of a throat snagged his attention away from Andri. His mother walked further into the room and settled lightly on the sofa. Travis didn't mind the distraction too much. His mother had changed in the last year. Not as much as he'd hoped, of course. She was still cool and a bit distant much of the time, but he understood now that's who she was. But he'd developed a loving connection with her that still surprised him some days. He'd caught glimpses of the garden in her, the free, fun woman inside the elegant, controlled exterior, and he found happiness in that.

Sophia looked at her tablet, sliding her finger to navigate the screens. "I apologize for interrupting, my dears, but if we don't finalize the last of these details, you will literally be late for your own wedding."

When his mother had offered to be their wedding planner, it seemed like the obvious choice. She loved planning events, handling their wedding had brought a delight to her eyes he'd never seen before, and she'd taken care of details Travis, and so far Andri, too, would never have thought about. But he hadn't anticipated that in her formidable hands, his idea of an intimate, understated event would be tossed aside in favor of a Sophia Holt-level soiree. Luckily, she'd agreed to a firm two hundred guest limit. Most of that number were family.

Andri turned to face his mother, grinning as they went over last minute planning. When they finished, Sophia rose to help get Zoe's dinner on the table. Travis held Andri back. He heard the front door open, announcing Rachel's arrival. Danny was reading in Dad's old office, so someone would have to call him to dinner.

For the moment, though, he and his bride-to-be were alone. He pressed his lips against her cheek. "I love you."

She looked at him, tracing her fingertips along his jaw. "Love you, too."

"Can't wait to marry you."

"Me too."

"Wish we'd eloped."

She giggled. "Me too."

Travis gently pulled on her ponytail until she arched her neck. He kissed the heated skin over her throat and she threaded her fingers into his hair. "Can't wait to get you back in my bed for the night where you belong," he whispered against her skin.

She groaned. "Two more weeks."

Two weeks of sneaky sex and then they'd be married and Zoe would head back to Phoenix. It would be the longest fourteen days of his entire life.

Andri kissed his lips, then laughed softly. "Are you ever going to tell Ma that you don't like baklava?"

He shook his head. "And have her realize I'm not the perfect son-in-law? No way."

About The Author

Lucy Francis grew up with characters living in her head, clamoring for attention. Whether those characters were elves, knights, aliens or earthlings, she listened and wrote their tales, which always included love. She still listens, plays matchmaker, and scribbles the resulting stories. Lucy has lived all over the United States, but calls Utah home. She lives with her husband, five children, and a pet menagerie that once included nine different species. She loves horses, fixing broken things, British TV shows, and tending the urban forest she planted in her front yard.

Visit Lucy Francis at:

www.lucyfrancis.net

www.facebook.com/lucyfrancisauthor

www.goodreads.com/lucyfrancis

Email: kissybooks@yahoo.com

Twitter: @LucysKissyBooks

Watch for Rachel's story, Seeking Shelter,
coming Spring, 2013.

Also available:

Mending Fences

By Lucy Francis

She was the first woman to turn him down.

Businessman-turned-rancher Curran Shaw is no stranger to
hard work, but women have never required much effort. When
a mysterious brunette at a resort-town Halloween party sparks
his interest and then vanishes, he vows to finish what she
started. It's finding her that's going to be the hard part.

He was her fantasy, and that's all he could ever be.

Victoria Linden has reconstructed her life and soul from the
devastation wrought by an abusive ex and her own failures. She
desperately wants to be loved, but what man will agree to the
control and limitations she needs in order to hold herself
together? Especially a man like Curran, who's used to getting
whatever he wants. Walking away from him after a searing kiss
is her only option.

When serendipity brings them together in the snowy
mountains of Utah, will Victoria and Curran be able to mend
the fences in their hearts, or will discovery and heartbreak tear
them apart?